GREGOR AND THE
PROPHECY OF BANE

ALSO BY SUZANNE COLLINS:

The Underland Chronicles:

Gregor the Overlander
BOOK 1

Gregor and the Prophecy of Bane
BOOK 2

Gregor and the Curse of the Warmbloods
BOOK 3

Gregor and the Marks of Secret
BOOK 4

Gregor and the Code of Claw
BOOK 5

The Hunger Games Trilogy:

The Hunger Games
Catching Fire
Mockingjay

GREGOR AND THE
PROPHECY OF BANE

BOOK 2 IN THE *NEW YORK TIMES*
BESTSELLING UNDERLAND CHRONICLES

SUZANNE COLLINS

SCHOLASTIC INC.

No part of this publication may be reproduced, stored in a retrieval system, or transmitted in any form or by any means, electronic, mechanical, photocopying, recording, or otherwise, without written permission of the publisher. For information regarding permission, write to Scholastic Inc., Attention: Permissions Department, 557 Broadway, New York, NY 10012.

This book was originally published in hardcover by Scholastic Press in 2004.

ISBN 978-0-439-65076-2

25 24 23 22   15 16 17 18/0

Printed in the U.S.A.   40

This edition first printing, July 2013

The text was set in 12-pt. Sabon.

For Cap

PART 1
The Mission

CHAPTER

1

When Gregor opened his eyes he had the distinct impression that someone was watching him. He glanced around his tiny bedroom, trying to keep as still as possible. The ceiling was empty. Nothing on his dresser. Then he saw it sitting on the windowsill, motionless except for the delicate twitching of its antennas. A cockroach.

"You're just looking for trouble," he said softly to the cockroach. "You want my mom to see you?"

The cockroach rubbed its feelers together but made no attempt to run away. Gregor sighed. He reached for an old mayonnaise jar that held his pencils, emptied it on the bed, and in one swift move trapped the cockroach beneath it.

He didn't even have to get up to do it. His bedroom wasn't actually a bedroom. Probably it was supposed to be some kind of storage space. Gregor's single bed was wedged into it so, at night, he came in the doorway and crawled straight up to his pillow. On the wall facing the foot of the bed, there was a little alcove with just enough room for a narrow dresser, although you could only open the drawers about eight inches. He had to do his homework sitting cross-legged on his bed with a board on his knees. And there was no door. But Gregor wasn't complaining. He had a window that looked out on the street, the ceilings were nice and high, and he had more privacy than anybody else in the apartment. No one came in his room much . . . if you didn't count the roaches.

What was it with the roaches lately, anyway? They'd always had some in the apartment, but now it seemed like every time he turned around he'd spot one. Not running. Not trying to hide. Just sitting there . . . watching him. It was weird. And it was a lot of work trying to keep them alive.

This past summer when a giant roach had sacrificed herself to save his two-year-old sister Boots's life miles beneath the city of New York, he'd vowed never to kill another one of the bugs. But if his mom saw them, man, they were goners. It was up to Gregor to get them out of the apartment before her roach radar kicked in. When it was warm out, he'd just trapped them and put them out on the fire escape. But he was afraid the bugs would freeze now that it was December, so lately he'd been trying to stick them as far down in the kitchen trash as he could manage. He thought they'd be happy there.

Gregor nudged the roach off the sill and up the side of the mayonnaise jar. He crept down the hallway past the bathroom, past the bedroom that Boots, his seven-year-old-sister, Lizzie, and his grandma shared, and into the living room. His mom was gone already. She must've taken the breakfast shift at the coffee shop where she waited tables on weekends. She worked full-time as a dentist's receptionist during the week, but lately they needed every penny.

Gregor's dad lay on the pull-out couch. Even when he was asleep he wasn't still. His fingers twitched and plucked fitfully at his blanket, and he was muttering softly. His dad. His poor dad . . .

After being held prisoner by huge, vicious rats far beneath New York City for over two and a half years,

3

his dad was a wreck. During his stay in the Underland, which was what the inhabitants called it, he'd been starved, deprived of light, and physically abused in ways he would never discuss. He was tormented by nightmares and at times he had trouble separating reality from illusion even when he was awake. This was worse when he was feverish, which was often, because despite repeated trips to the doctor, he could not shake off a strange illness he'd brought back from the Underland.

Before Gregor had fallen after Boots through a grate in the laundry room and helped rescue his dad, he'd always thought that everything would be simple once his family was reunited. It was a thousand times better having his dad back, Gregor knew that. But it was not simple.

Gregor moved quietly into the kitchen and slid the roach into the trash. He set the jar on the counter and noticed it was bare. The fridge held half a carton of milk, a gallon bottle of apple juice with maybe one glassful in it, and a jar of mustard. Gregor braced himself and opened the cabinet. Half a loaf of bread, some peanut butter, and a box of oatmeal. He gave the box of oatmeal a shake and exhaled in relief. There was enough food for breakfast and lunch. And since it was Saturday, Gregor wouldn't even need to eat at home. He'd be going over to help Mrs. Cormaci.

Mrs. Cormaci. It was strange how in a few short months she had changed from being their nosy neighbor into a kind of guardian angel. Shortly after Gregor, Boots, and their dad had returned from the Underland, he'd run into her in the hallway.

"So, where've you been, Mister?" she asked him. "Besides scaring the whole building to death." Gregor had given her the story his family had agreed upon: On the day he'd disappeared from the laundry room, he'd taken Boots out to the playground to play for a few minutes. They'd run into his dad, who was on his way to see his sick uncle in Virginia and wanted to take the kids with him. Gregor thought his dad had called his mom; his dad thought Gregor had called his mom; it wasn't until they got back that they realized what a crisis they'd caused.

"Hmph," said Mrs. Cormaci, giving him a hard look. "I thought your father was living in California."

"He was," said Gregor. "But now he's back with us."

"I see," Mrs. Cormaci again. "So, that's your story?"

Gregor nodded, knowing it was pretty lame.

"Hmph," said Mrs. Cormaci again. "Well, I'd work on that if I were you." And she walked off without another word.

Gregor thought she was mad at them, but a few days later she'd knocked on the door with a coffee cake. "I brought your father a coffee cake," she said. "It's a welcome-home thing. Is he here?"

He hadn't wanted to let her in, but his dad called out in a false, cheerful voice, "Is that Mrs. Cormaci?" and she'd bustled right in with her cake. The sight of his dad — bone thin, white-haired, hunched over on the couch — pulled her up short. If she had planned to interrogate him, she let it go right there. Instead, she exchanged a few comments about the weather and left.

Then, a couple of weeks after school started, his mom came in one evening with some news. "Mrs. Cormaci wants to hire you to help her on Saturdays," she said.

"Help her?" Gregor asked warily. "Help her do what?" He didn't want to help Mrs. Cormaci. She'd ask him a bunch of questions and probably want to read his future with her deck of tarot cards and —

"I don't know. Help her around her apartment. You don't have to do it if you don't want to. But I thought it might be a nice way for you to make some pocket money," said his mom.

And Gregor knew then that he would do it and forget about pocket money, forget about money for movies and comic books and stuff. He'd use the money for his family. Because even though his dad was home, there was no way he could go back to his job as a science teacher. He had only left the apartment a few times, and that was to go to the doctor. The six of them were living on what his mom could make. And with the medical bills, and school supplies, and clothes and food and rent and every other thing you had to have to live, it wasn't stretching far enough.

"What time does she want me there?" asked Gregor.

"She said ten would be good," said his mom.

That first Saturday, several months ago, there hadn't been much food in the apartment, either, so Gregor had just gulped down a couple of glasses of water and headed over to Mrs. Cormaci's. When she opened the door, the rich smell of something amazing hit him, filling his mouth with so much saliva that he had to swallow hard before he said hi.

"Oh, good, you came," said Mrs. Cormaci. "Follow me."

7

Feeling awkward, Gregor followed her into her kitchen. A gigantic pot of sauce was bubbling away on the stove. Another pot contained lasagna noodles. Piles of vegetables covered the counter. "There's a fund-raiser tonight at my church and I said I'd bring lasagna. Don't ask me why." Mrs. Cormaci dumped several ladles of sauce into a bowl, stuck a big wedge of bread in it, clunked it on the table, and pushed Gregor into a chair before it. "Taste it."

Gregor looked at her, unsure.

"Taste it! I have to know if it's fit to be served," insisted Mrs. Cormaci.

He dipped the bread into the sauce and took a bite. It was so good, his eyes watered. "Boy," he said, when he had swallowed.

"You hate it. It's revolting. I should throw the whole pot out and go buy jar sauce from the grocery," said Mrs. Cormaci.

"No!" said Gregor, alarmed. "No. It's the best sauce I ever tasted!"

Mrs. Cormaci slapped a spoon down beside him. "Then eat it and wash your hands, with soap, because you've got chopping to do."

After he'd inhaled the sauce and bread, she set him to work chopping piles of vegetables that she sautéed in olive oil. He mixed eggs and spices into ricotta cheese. They layered big, flat noodles and cheese and sauce and vegetables into three enormous pans. He helped her wash up, and she declared it was time for lunch.

They had tuna salad sandwiches in her dining room while Mrs. Cormaci talked about her three kids, who were all grown and lived in different states, and Mr. Cormaci, who'd passed away five years ago. Gregor vaguely remembered him as a nice man who had given him quarters and, one time, a baseball card. "Not a day goes by that I don't miss him," said Mrs. Cormaci. Then she brought out a pound cake.

After lunch, Gregor helped her clean out a closet and carried a few boxes down to her storage space. At two o'clock, she said he was done. She had not asked any questions about him except how he liked school. She sent him out the door with forty bucks, a winter coat that had belonged to her daughter when she was little, and a lasagna. When he tried to object, she just said, "I can't take three lasagnas to the fund-raiser. People take two. You walk in with three and everybody thinks you're a big show-off. And what? I'm going to eat it? With my cholesterol? Take it. Eat it. Go. I'll see you next Saturday." And she closed the door in his face.

It was too much. All of it. But he could surprise his mom and buy groceries and maybe some lightbulbs since three lamps were out in the house. Lizzie needed a coat. And the lasagna . . . somehow that was the best part of all. Suddenly he wanted to knock on the door and tell Mrs. Cormaci the truth about the Underland and everything that had happened and that he was sorry that he had lied to her. But he couldn't. . . .

Gregor was jolted out of his memory when Lizzie padded into the kitchen in her pajamas. She was small for her age, but the look of concern on her face made her look older than seven. "Is there any food for today?" she asked.

"Sure, there's plenty," said Gregor, trying to sound like he hadn't been worried himself. "Look, you guys can have this oatmeal for breakfast, and peanut butter sandwiches for lunch. I'll go ahead and make the oatmeal now."

Lizzie wasn't allowed to use the stove, but she opened the cabinet with the bowls. She counted out four and then hesitated. "Are you eating breakfast or —?"

"Nah, I'm not even hungry this morning," he said, even though his stomach was growling. "Besides, I'm going over to help Mrs. Cormaci."

"Are we going sledding later?" she asked.

Gregor nodded. "Uh-huh. I'll take you and Boots over to Central Park. If dad's okay."

They had found a plastic snow saucer out by the trash. It had a big crack in it, but their dad had mended it with duct tape. Gregor had been promising to take his sisters sledding all week. But if his dad had a fever, someone needed to stay home with him and their grandma, who spent a lot of her time thinking she was on her family's farm in Virginia. And afternoons were usually when the fever hit.

"If he's not, I'll stay home. You can take Boots," said Lizzie.

He knew she was dying to go. She was only seven. Why did things have to be so hard for her?

Gregor spent the next few hours helping Mrs. Cormaci make big glass casserole dishes of scalloped potatoes, polishing her odd collection of antique clocks, and getting her Christmas decorations out of the storage space. When she asked Gregor what he was hoping to get for Christmas, he just shrugged.

When he left that day, along with the money and a vat of scalloped potatoes, Mrs. Cormaci gave him something wonderful. It was a pair of her son's old work boots. They were a little worn and a little too big, but they were sturdy and waterproof and laced up above his ankles. The sneakers Gregor was wearing, which were his only pair of shoes, were starting to split at the toe and sometimes, after walking through the slushy streets, his feet would be wet all day at school.

"Are you sure he doesn't want these?" said Gregor.

"My son? Sure he wants them. He wants them to sit in my closet taking up space so he can come back once a year and say, 'Hey, there's my old boots,' and stuff them back in the closet. If I trip over those boots getting to my iron one more time, I'll disown him. Get them out of here before I throw them out the window!" Mrs. Cormaci said with a wave of contempt at the boots. "I'll see you next Saturday."

When he got home, it was clear his dad wasn't feeling well.

"You kids go on. Go sledding. I'll be fine here with Grandma," he said, but his teeth were chattering from chills.

Boots was dancing around with the plastic saucer on her head. "Go sedding? We go sedding, Ge-go?"

"I'll stay," Lizzie whispered to Gregor. "But could you get some of that fever medicine before you go? We ran out yesterday."

Gregor considered staying as well, but Boots hardly ever got out, and Lizzie was too young to take her sledding alone.

He ran down to the drugstore and bought a bottle of pills that brought down your fever. On the way home he stopped at a table where a man sold used books on the street. A few days ago, walking by, he had noticed a paperback puzzle book. It was kind of beat up, but when Gregor flipped through it he saw that only one or two of the puzzles had been done. The man gave it to him for a buck. Lastly, he picked up a couple of navel oranges, the expensive kind with the really thick skin. Lizzie loved those.

Lizzie's little face lit up when he gave her the book. "Oh! Oh, I'll get a pencil!" she said, and ran off. She was nuts about puzzles. Math puzzles, word puzzles, any kind. And even though she was seven, she could do a lot of the ones meant for adults. When she was a tiny kid you'd take her out and see a stop sign and

13

she'd go, "Stop, pots, spot, tops . . ." She'd instantly rearrange all the letters into all the words she could think of. Like she couldn't help it.

When Gregor had told her about the Underland, she gave a little gasp when he'd mentioned the horrible rat king, Gorger. "Gorger! That's the same as your name, Gregor!" She didn't mean the same name, she meant you could mix around the letters in Gorger and spell Gregor. Who else would notice that?

So he felt okay when he left her. Their grandma was asleep, his dad had medicine, and Lizzie was curled up in a chair next to him sucking on an orange slice and happily cracking a cryptogram.

Boots's excitement was so contagious that Gregor felt happy, too. He'd put on an extra pair of socks and stuffed the toes of his new boots with toilet paper so his feet were warm and snug and dry. His family had enough scalloped potatoes at home for a small army. A light snow was gently spinning down around them, and they were going sledding. For the moment, things were okay.

They rode the subway to Central Park, where there was a great sledding hill. Lots of people were there, some with fancy sleds, some with beat-up old saucers.

One guy was just sliding down on a big trash bag. Boots squealed in delight every time they went down the hill and as soon as they slid to a stop, she shouted, "More, Ge-go. More!" They sledded until the light began to fade. Near an exit to the street, Gregor stopped for a while to let Boots play. He leaned against a tree while she fascinated herself by making footprints in the snow.

The park felt like Christmas with all the sledding and the pine trees and the funny, lumpy snowmen that kids had built. Big, shimmery stars hung from the lamp-posts. People walked by with shopping bags that sported reindeer and poinsettia. Gregor should have felt cheerful, but instead, Christmas made him feel anxious.

His family didn't have any money. It didn't matter so much for him. He was eleven. But Boots and Lizzie were little, and it should be fun, it should be magical, with a Christmas tree and presents and stockings on the coat hooks (which is where they hung theirs because they didn't have a chimney) and nice things to eat.

Gregor had been trying to save some money out of what Mrs. Cormaci gave him, but it always seemed to go for something else, like fever medicine or milk or diapers. Boots could really go through a lot of diapers. She probably needed one now, but he hadn't brought any, so they had to get going.

"Boots!" Gregor called. "Time to go!" He looked around the park and saw that the lamps that lined the paths had come on. Daylight was almost gone. "Boots! Let's go!" he said. He stepped out from the tree, turned in a circle, and felt a jolt of alarm.

In the brief time he'd been thinking, Boots had vanished.

CHAPTER

2

"Boots!" Gregor was beginning to panic. She'd been right here a minute ago. Hadn't she? Or had he been so busy thinking, he'd lost track of how much time had passed? "Boots!"

Where could she have gone? Into the trees? Out onto the street? What if someone had taken her? "Boots!"

There wasn't even anyone around to ask. The park had emptied out as dark had fallen. Struggling to stay calm, Gregor tried to follow the trail of footprints that she'd been making in the snow. But there were so many footprints! And he could barely see!

Suddenly he heard a dog barking nearby. Maybe it had found Boots, or at least its owner might have seen her. Gregor ran through the trees to a small clearing somewhat illuminated by a nearby light. A feisty little terrier was running in a circle around a stick, barking its head off. Intermittently it would grab the stick in its jaws, give it a good shake, and drop it on the ground. Then it would begin its frantic barking again.

A pretty woman, dressed in winter jogging clothes, appeared. "Petey! Petey! What are you doing?" She scooped up the dog and shook her head at Gregor as she walked off. "Sorry, he goes a little crazy sometimes."

But Gregor didn't respond. He was staring at the stick, or what he'd thought was a stick, that had been driving the dog wild. It was smooth and shiny and black. He picked it up and it bent in two. Not like a broken stick. But like a leg. An insect leg. From a giant roach . . .

His head whipped around the area. When they had returned from the Underland that summer, they had come up through a series of tunnels that led to Central Park. They had been near the street, just as he was now.

There, on the ground. That big slab of rock. It had been moved recently — he could tell by the marks in the snow — and then moved back into place. Something red was trapped under the edge of the rock. He pulled it out. It was Boots's mitten.

The giant roaches from the Underland had idolized Boots. They'd called her the princess and done some special ritual dance to honor her. And now they'd kidnapped her right out from under his nose.

"Boots . . . ," he said softly. But he knew she couldn't hear him at this point.

He pulled out his cell phone. They couldn't afford a cell phone, but after three members of her family had mysteriously disappeared, his mother had insisted they get one, anyway. He dialed home. His dad answered.

"Dad? It's Gregor. Look, something happened. Something bad. I'm in Central Park, near that place where we came up this summer, and the roaches, you know, the giant ones? They were here and they took Boots. I wasn't watching her close enough, it's my fault and . . . I have to go back down!" Gregor knew he had to hurry.

"But . . . Gregor . . ." His dad's voice was full of confusion and fear. "You can't —"

"I have to, Dad. Or we might not ever see her again. You know how crazy the roaches are about her. Look, don't let Mom call the police this time. There's nothing they can do. If I'm not back right away, tell people we've got the flu or something, okay?"

"Listen, stay there. I'm coming with you. I'll be there as quick as I can," said his dad. Gregor could hear him panting as he tried to struggle to his feet.

"No, Dad! No, you'd never make it. You can't even walk down the block!" said Gregor.

"But I . . . but I can't let you . . ." He could hear his dad beginning to cry.

"Don't worry. I'll be okay. I mean, I've been down there before. But I got to go, Dad, or they'll get too far." Gregor puffed as he struggled to slide away the slab of rock.

"Gregor? You have any light?" asked his dad.

"No!" said Gregor. This was a real problem. "Wait, yes! Yes!" Mrs. Cormaci had given him a mini flashlight in case the lights ever went out when he was on the subway. He had clipped it to his key ring. "I've got a flashlight. Dad, I've got to go now."

"I know, son. Gregor . . . I love you." His dad's voice was shaking. "Be careful, okay?"

"I will be. Love you, too. I'll see you soon, okay?" said Gregor.

"See you soon," his dad whispered hoarsely.

And then Gregor lowered himself down into the hole. He stuck the phone in one pocket and pulled out his key ring from another. When he clicked on the little flashlight, he was surprised by the amount of light it produced. He slid the rock slab closed and started down a long, steep flight of steps.

As he got to the bottom he stopped and closed his eyes for a minute, trying to re-create in his head the path that had brought him here last summer. They had been flying then, on the back of a big black bat named Ares, who was his bond. In the Underland, a human and a bat could take a vow and swear always to protect each other no matter how desperate the situation. Then the two were called bonds.

Ares had flown Gregor, Boots, and his dad back from the Underland and left them at the foot of the stairs and headed off to the . . . right! Gregor was pretty sure it had been to the right, so he started running that way.

The tunnel was cold and dank and desolate. It had been made by people — regular people, not the violet-eyed, pale Underlanders he had met deep in the earth — but Gregor felt sure that it had been for-gotten by New Yorkers long ago.

His flashlight beam caught a mouse, and it skittered away in terror. Light didn't come down here. People didn't come down here. What was *he* doing down here?

"I can't believe it," thought Gregor. "I can't believe I have to go back down — *there*!" Back into the strange dark land of giant roaches and spiders and, worst of all, rats! The thought of seeing one of those six-foot sneering, fanged creatures filled him with dread.

Boy, his mom was not going to like this.

Last summer, when they'd finally come home late one night, she'd freaked out. First her two missing kids show up with their missing dad, who can barely walk, and then they all sit down and tell her some bizarre story about a land miles under the earth.

Gregor could tell she didn't believe them at first. Well, who would? But it was Boots's chatter that she couldn't ignore.

"Beeg bugs, Mama! I like beeg bugs! We go ride!" Boots had said, happily bouncing on her mother's lap. "I ride bat. Ge-go ride bat."

"Did you see a rat, baby?" her mom said softly.

"Rat bad," Boots said with a frown. And Gregor remembered this was the exact phrase he had heard the roaches use to describe the rats. They were bad. Very bad. Well, most of them . . .

They'd told the story three times, under intense questioning from his mom. They'd showed her their strange Underland clothing woven by the huge spiders that lived there. Then there was his dad, white-haired, shaking, emaciated.

At dawn, she'd decided to believe them. At one minute after dawn, she was down in the laundry room nailing, screwing, gluing, doing everything she could to seal shut the grate they'd all fallen through. She and Gregor shoved a dryer closer to it. Not enough so it would draw a lot of attention. But enough so that no one could get back there and open it up.

Then she put the laundry room off-limits. No one was allowed down there, ever. So, once a week Gregor helped her haul the laundry three blocks to use a Laundromat.

But his mom hadn't thought about this entrance in Central Park. And neither had he. Until now.

The tunnel came to a fork. He hesitated a minute, and then headed off to the left, hoping it was the right direction. As he jogged along, the tunnel began to change. The bricks left off, and natural stone walls took over.

Gregor went down one last flight of steps. This one was carved out of natural stone. It looked really old. He guessed it must have been made by the Underlanders hundreds of years earlier, when they'd begun their descent to make a new world deep in the earth.

The tunnels began to twist and turn, and soon Gregor lost his bearings. What if he was just getting totally lost in some maze of tunnels while the roaches carried Boots off in a completely different direction? What if he'd taken a wrong turn back at the stairs ... what if ... no, there! His flashlight landed on a spot of red on the ground, and Gregor picked up Boots's second mitten. She could never hold on to them. Luckily.

As Gregor sprinted off, he began to notice a crunching sound under his feet. Shining the flashlight onto the floor, he realized it was covered with a variety of small insects scurrying down the tunnel as fast as they could.

As he stopped to investigate the situation, something skittered over his boot. A mouse. There were dozens running past him. And there by the wall — hadn't he just seen some kind of molelike animal go by? The whole floor was alive with creatures headed in Gregor's direction in a big, creepy stampede. They weren't trying to eat one another. They weren't fighting. They were just running, the way he had seen animals on the news one time running from a forest fire. They were afraid of something. But of what?

Gregor shot the beam of his flashlight behind him and there was his answer. About fifty yards away, galloping toward him, were two rats. The Underland kind.

Gregor turned on his heel and ran. "Oh, geez!" he gasped. "What are they doing here?" Cockroaches had taken Boots. He'd seen one of their legs. But what were Underland rats doing so close to the surface of the earth?

Well, that was something to figure out later, because he had bigger issues at the moment. The rats were gaining on him, and gaining on him fast. He tried to think of a plan, but nothing came to mind. He couldn't outrun them; he couldn't outclimb them; and he sure couldn't outfight them with their six-inch teeth and razor-sharp claws and —

"Ugh!" He ran smack into the side of something hard. It caught him stomach high, knocking the wind out of him. He dropped the flashlight, but as it fell into empty space, Gregor recognized the circular stone opening that Ares had squeezed through to bring them home. Somewhere far, far below lay a massive Underland ocean. The Waterway.

Without thinking, Gregor swung his leg over the side of the circle and lowered himself down inside. His fingers clung to the edge as his legs swung free. "Maybe the rats won't see me inside here," he thought, and immediately the stupidity of what he'd done hit him. The rats didn't need to *see* anything. The rats navigated by their incredible sense of smell. So what might have been a really decent hiding place if you were being chased by people was utterly worthless if you were trying to lose rats.

Yep, and here they were. He could hear their claws screeching to a halt on the stone, then their panting, and then their confusion.

"What's he doing?" growled one.

"No idea," said the second.

For a few moments, Gregor could hear nothing but the pounding of his own heart. Then the second voice sputtered, "Oh, oh, you don't suppose he's hiding, do you?"

And that's when they started laughing. It was a nasty, raspy laugh.

"Come out, come out, wherever you are!" said the first voice, and the rats cracked up again. Gregor couldn't see them, but he felt pretty sure they were rolling around on the ground.

He had two choices. Climb back out and face the rats in pitch blackness, or drop into the darkness below and hope against hope that some Underlander scout found him before he drowned or became something's dinner.

He was trying to weigh the odds of surviving. Either way they were very low. Either way the likelihood of finding Boots and bringing her home was —

"Drop, Overlander," purred a voice. For a second he thought it was the rats, but it couldn't be because they were still laughing and, anyway, it didn't sound like them. It sounded like —

"Drop, Overlander," said the voice again, and this time the rats heard it, too. He could sense them springing to their feet.

"Kill him!" snarled the first, and as its hot, ratty breath hit his fingers, Gregor stopped weighing his odds and let go.

He could hear the scrape of claws on the stone ledge he had been clinging to moments before, along with a volley of strange rat curses.

Then the sickening sense of free-falling through space consumed him. He had fallen like this twice before, once when he'd gone down the grate in his laundry room after Boots, and once when he'd leaped into a huge void when he was trying to save his dad and sister and friends. "This," he thought, "is something I'm never going to get used to."

Where was Ares? That was Ares's voice he'd heard, wasn't it? For a second Gregor thought he'd imagined hearing the bat, but then he remembered the rats had reacted to the sound, too.

"Ares!" he called out. The darkness absorbed his voice like a towel. "Ares!"

"Ooph!" Gregor said, more in surprise than anything, because suddenly the bat was under him and he was riding, not falling, through the darkness.

"Man, am I glad you showed up!" said Gregor, his hands clinging to the thick fur on Ares's neck.

"I am glad you are here also, Overlander," said Ares. "I am sorry you had to fall this far. I know this causes you discomfort, but I was retrieving your light stick."

"My light stick?" said Gregor.

"Behind you," said Ares.

Gregor turned around and saw a faint glow behind him. He picked up his mini flashlight that had been shining into the fur on Ares's back. "Thanks!" The light calmed him down a little.

"Man, you'll never guess what happened! Those cockroaches came up in the park and took Boots! They just stole her right out from under my nose!" And suddenly Gregor was really mad at the roaches. "I mean, what were they thinking? Did they think I wouldn't notice?"

Ares veered off to the right and began to fly over a ridge along one side of the Waterway. "No, Overlander, they —"

"Well, did they think I wouldn't care? Like it would be okay just to grab her and run and I'd be, like, 'Oh, well, guess I won't be seeing Boots around.'"

"They did not think that," said Ares.

"Did they think I wouldn't come get her? And they'd just be able to keep her and do their little dances around her and sing 'Patty Cake' and —" said Gregor.

"The crawlers knew you would follow," Ares slipped in, before Gregor lost it.

"Of course, I followed! And man, when I get hold of those bugs, they'd better have some really good explanation for this whole thing. How far are we from their place?" said Gregor.

"Several hours. But I am taking you to Regalia," said Ares.

"Regalia? I don't want to go to Regalia!" said Gregor. "You take me to the roaches, and you take me there now!" ordered Gregor.

Thwack!

Gregor landed flat on his back. Ares had flipped him over onto the stone ridge. Before he could speak, the bat was on his chest, his claws digging deep into his down jacket.

Ares's face was just inches from Gregor's. The bat's gums were pulled back over his teeth in a snarl. "I do not take orders from you, Overlander. Let us be clear on this from the start. I do not take orders from you!"

"Whoa!" said Gregor, startled by Ares's intensity. "What's your problem?"

"My problem is that at this moment, you are reminding me a great deal of Henry," said Ares.

This was really the first time Gregor had ever gotten a good look at Ares's face. The light in the Underland was usually dim. And Ares was particularly hard to see because of his uniform blackness, black eyes, black nose, black mouth set in his black fur. But in the direct beam of the flashlight, he could see the bat was furious.

Ares had saved his life. Gregor had kept Ares from banishment, which would have meant certain death. They were bonded together and had sworn to fight to the death for each other. But they had never exchanged more than a handful of words. As Ares glared down at him, Gregor realized he knew next to nothing about the bat.

"Henry?" said Gregor, because he couldn't think of anything else to say.

"Yes, Henry. My old bond. You remember, I let him smash to his death on the rocks so that I could give you more time," Ares said almost sarcastically. "And right now I am wondering if I should not have let you both fall because, like Henry, you are under the impression that I am your servant."

"No, I'm not!" objected Gregor. "Look, we don't even have servants where I come from. I just wanted to go get my sister!"

"And I am trying to unite you with your sister as

quickly as I can. But, like Henry, you do not listen to me," said Ares.

Gregor had to admit this was true. He'd kept talking right over Ares every time the bat had tried to speak. But he didn't like being compared with Henry. He was nothing like that traitor. Still, maybe he *had* been out of line.

"Okay, I'm sorry. I was mad and I should have listened to you. Now get off my chest," said Gregor.

"Get off my chest, what?" said Ares.

"Get off my chest now!" said Gregor, getting angry again.

"Try again," said Ares. "Because to me this sounds very much like an order."

Gregor gritted his teeth and suppressed an impulse to push the bat off. "Get — off — my — chest *please*."

Ares considered the request for a moment, decided it was satisfactory, and fluttered off to the side.

Gregor sat up and rubbed his chest. He was unharmed, but there were several deep holes in his jacket where Ares's claws had pierced the fabric.

"Hey! Can you watch those claws? Look what you did to my jacket!" said Gregor.

"It is of no matter. They will burn it, anyway," Ares said indifferently.

It was at that moment that Gregor decided he was bonded to a big jerk. And he felt pretty sure that Ares had come to the same conclusion.

"Okay," Gregor said coldly. "So, we have to go to Regalia. Why?"

"That is where the crawlers are taking your sister," said Ares, matching Gregor's tone.

"And why would the crawlers want to take my sister to Regalia?" asked Gregor.

"Because," said Ares, "the rats have sworn to kill her."

CHAPTER

4

"Kill her? But why?" asked Gregor, stunned.

"It is foretold by 'The Prophecy of Bane,'" said Ares.

"The Prophecy of Bane." Gregor remembered it now. When he had left the Underland the first time, he had told Luxa he would never come back, and she had said, "That is not what it says in 'The Prophecy of Bane.'" And then he'd tried to ask Vikus about it, but the old man had been evasive and hustled him onto his bat and given the command to leave. So, Gregor didn't know what it meant, but the first prophecy in which he'd been mentioned had resulted in the deaths of four members of a twelve-party quest and had triggered a war that had killed countless others.

A feeling of dread swept over him. "What does it say, Ares?"

"Ask Vikus," Ares said shortly. "I am tired of being interrupted."

He climbed on Ares's back, and they flew back to Regalia without exchanging another word. Gregor was angry with Ares but even angrier with himself for placing his family in jeopardy again. Yes, Luxa had mentioned "The Prophecy of Bane." It was just that once he and his mom had blocked that grate in the laundry room, Gregor had put the idea of returning to the Underland out of his mind. "Avoid the laundry room, avoid the Underland," he'd reasoned. But how could he have taken Boots to Central Park? He knew about the entrance there! He knew there was a second prophecy! It had been foolish to think it would be safe.

When they reached the beautiful stone city, it was so quiet that Gregor thought it must be nighttime here. Well, nighttime was relative, since the Underland had no sun or moon, no day or night, like the Overland. But Gregor figured it must be the time when most of the city was asleep.

Ares headed for the palace and made a smooth

landing in the High Hall, the big, ceiling-less room that could accommodate the arrival of many bats.

Standing patiently, all alone, was Vikus. The old man looked exactly as Gregor remembered him, his silver hair and beard trimmed very short, his violet eyes in a web of wrinkles that was mostly noticeable when he smiled. He was smiling now, as Gregor dismounted.

"Hey, Vikus," said Gregor.

"Ah, Gregor the Overlander! Ares has found you. I thought it would be best to seek you in the passage from your laundry room, but he insisted on scouting the Waterway. I ascertain that, as bonds, you already think alike," said Vikus.

Neither Ares nor Gregor responded. Since they weren't actually speaking to each other, it seemed stupid to act like they had some special mental link.

Vikus glanced from one to the other and then continued. "So . . . welcome! You look well. And your family?"

"Fine, thanks. Where's Boots?" said Gregor. He liked Vikus, but this whole situation with the roaches kidnapping Boots and the threat from the prophecy killed his mood for small talk.

"Ah, the crawlers should arrive with her shortly. Mareth led a party to meet them, and I could not dissuade Luxa from joining. By now, Ares has, of course, explained our predicament to you," said Vikus.

"Not really," said Gregor.

Vikus looked at each of them again, but neither Gregor nor Ares elaborated.

"Well, then. To begin with, we should examine together 'The Prophecy of Bane.' Perhaps you remember, when you were departing the Underland, I made some small mention of it," said Vikus.

"Very small," Gregor muttered. What he remembered was that Vikus had rushed him off and told him absolutely nothing.

"Let us proceed to Sandwich's room now. Ares, you will attend as well, please," Vikus said, and headed off into the palace.

Gregor followed him with Ares fluttering along behind.

Vikus did not resume the conversation until they'd reached a solid wooden door. He pulled a key from his cloak and turned it in the lock. The door swung open. "You will find it on your right," he said, and motioned for Gregor to enter ahead of him.

Gregor pulled a torch from a holder by the door and walked in to the room. It was entirely covered in tiny words carved into the stone walls in the 1600s by the founder of Regalia, Bartholomew of Sandwich. The words formed prophecies, visions of Sandwich's, that the Underlanders lived and died by. The first time Gregor had been in the room, the wall facing the door had been illuminated with a small oil lamp. That was where Sandwich had carved "The Prophecy of Gray." Now that area was in shadow. The lamp had been moved to the wall on his right. Above it was what looked like a poem. This must be it. "The Prophecy of Bane."

Gregor lifted his torch to get a clearer view and began to read:

> IF UNDER FELL, IF OVER LEAPED,
> IF LIFE WAS DEATH, IF DEATH LIFE REAPED,
> SOMETHING RISES FROM THE GLOOM
> TO MAKE THE UNDERLAND A TOMB.
>
> HEAR IT SCRATCHING DOWN BELOW,
> RAT OF LONG-FORGOTTEN SNOW,
> EVIL CLOAKED IN COAT OF WHITE
> WILL THE WARRIOR DRAIN YOUR LIGHT?

WHAT COULD TURN THE WARRIOR WEAK?

WHAT DO BURNING GNAWERS SEEK?

JUST A BARELY SPEAKING PUP

WHO HOLDS THE LAND OF UNDER UP.

DIE THE BABY, DIE HIS HEART,

DIE HIS MOST ESSENTIAL PART.

DIE THE PEACE THAT RULES THE HOUR.

GNAWERS HAVE THEIR KEY TO POWER.

Gregor didn't know what it meant any more than he had understood "The Prophecy of Gray." But his mind snagged on one phrase that chilled him to the bone: Die the baby . . . Die the baby . . . Die the baby . . . Boots . . .

"Okay, I want to go through this whole thing. Right here, right now," said Gregor.

Vikus nodded. "Yes, I think it wise we dissect the prophecy immediately. It is not as cryptic as the first, but there are things you must know. Shall we begin at the beginning?" He moved to the prophecy and brushed his fingers over the first two lines. "You have fresh eyes, whereas I have read this thousands of times. Tell me, Gregor, what make you of this?"

Gregor looked at the lines more closely this time . . .

If Under fell, if Over leaped,

If life was death, if death life reaped,

. . . and realized he did know what they meant. "It's about me and Henry. I'm the Over, I leaped. Henry's the Under, he fell. I lived, and he died."

"Yes, and King Gorger and his rats also died, reaping much life in the Underland," said Vikus.

"Hey, how come you didn't tell me about this before? Then maybe I would have known what was coming!" said Gregor.

"No, Gregor, it is clear only in hindsight. 'Under' could have referred not only to Henry, but to any other Underland creature, or the Underland itself. 'Over' could have been your father. Your leap may not have been a literal leap but a mental or spiritual leap. Henry's fall might have alluded to any variety of physical deaths, not to mention a fall from power or honor. In truth, a human Underlander literally falling to his death was not a popular interpretation. Henry never would have suspected he would die in such a way," said Vikus.

"Why not?" asked Gregor.

Vikus glanced at Ares and hesitated.

"Because he would have expected me to catch him," Ares said bluntly.

"Yes," said Vikus. "So, you see that the first prophecy was indeed gray to us, although now, of course, it seems as clear as water. Shall we go on?"

Gregor read the next bit to himself.

SOMETHING RISES FROM THE GLOOM
TO MAKE THE UNDERLAND A TOMB.

"So, something bad is coming. Something deadly," said Gregor.

"Not just coming. It is here, and has been here for some time. Only the rats have concealed it, even from their own. You will find more about it in the next stanza," Vikus said, gesturing to the next four lines.

HEAR IT SCRATCHING DOWN BELOW,
RAT OF LONG-FORGOTTEN SNOW,
EVIL CLOAKED IN COAT OF WHITE
WILL THE WARRIOR DRAIN YOUR LIGHT?

Gregor studied the lines for a minute. "It's a rat. A white rat?"

"The color of long-forgotten snow, for we do not get snow in the Underland. Although I imagine it to be very beautiful," Vikus said a bit wistfully.

"It is," said Gregor. "There's snow everywhere right now. It makes everything look better." It did, too, when it had just fallen. It covered up the dirt and the trash, and for a while the city looked clean and fresh. And then it turned to slush. "So, this white rat . . . ?"

"It is the stuff of legends. Even when he lived in the Overland, Sandwich knew tales of the white rat. Historically, one will appear every few centuries, gather other rats about it, and create a reign of terror. It is remarkable in cunning, strength, and size," said Vikus.

"Size?" said Gregor. "You mean it's even bigger than the other rats down here?"

"Considerably so," said Vikus. "As legend has it. And at this point in time, the only thing that stands between this creature and the Underland is you. The warrior. You are a threat to it. That is why the white rat has been so carefully concealed. The rats do not want you to find it. But you also have a vulnerability."

Vikus tapped the third stanza, and Gregor read on.

> WHAT COULD TURN THE WARRIOR WEAK?
> WHAT DO BURNING GNAWERS SEEK?
> JUST A BARELY SPEAKING PUP
> WHO HOLDS THE LAND OF UNDER UP.

"Do you know what is meant by 'pup'?" asked Vikus.

"Ripred called Luxa and Henry pups once, when they wouldn't obey him," said Gregor. And suddenly he wondered how much the large, scarred rat who had helped save his father knew about all this.

"He undoubtedly said it sarcastically, and to remind them he was in charge. For, to rats, a 'pup' is a baby. The only baby we know of who is close to you is Boots," said Vikus.

Gregor felt his eyes pulled to the last stanza of the prophecy.

> DIE THE BABY, DIE HIS HEART,
> DIE HIS MOST ESSENTIAL PART.
> DIE THE PEACE THAT RULES THE HOUR.
> GNAWERS HAVE THEIR KEY TO POWER.

"So, they think that if they" — Gregor could hardly say it — "kill Boots, something will happen to me."

"It will break you somehow," said Vikus. "And if that happens, the rats will overtake the rest of us."

"No pressure or anything," Gregor said, but he felt very scared. "You're sure it's Boots?"

"As sure as we may dare be. Your closeness to her is well known. That you sacrificed yourself, that you leaped rather than let King Gorger kill her — this made a great impression on everyone. Can you think of another baby it could be, Gregor?" Vikus asked solemnly.

Gregor shook his head. It was Boots. And they were right about one thing: If they killed her, something in him would break. "So, why did you bring her down here? Why didn't you just leave her in the Overland, where she was safe?"

"Because she was not safe. And neither were you. The crawlers watch you night and day, to protect you," said Vikus.

The roach he had trapped in the mayonnaise jar that morning flashed before his eyes. "You mean the little ones?"

"Yes, they are in communication with the larger ones below. But the rats watch you as well. They have been tracking your family's movements since shortly after you left the Underland, waiting for a chance to take your sister's life," said Vikus. "It was not possible in your home. But today you ventured out with her very near one of the gateways."

"We went sledding in Central Park," said Gregor.

Then Ares spoke up. "The Overlander was chased in the tunnels by gnawers. He had to drop into the Waterway to escape them."

"Then the crawlers must have rescued Boots just in time. She was the rats' target today, Gregor," said Vikus.

"Why not just kill me?" Gregor asked numbly.

"They would be happy to. But they have seen you leap and live to tell of it, so they are less confident in such a goal," answered Vikus. "And at the moment they are more concerned with the prophecy. It is by killing Boots that they mean to destroy you."

"I still think we would be safer in the Overland. We just won't go to Central Park. We'll keep Boots inside. . . ." But Gregor wasn't really sure it would be safer.

"I will send you back directly, if that is what you wish. But they will find her, Gregor, now that they are set on it. In their minds, it is a race. They must kill Boots before the white rat is killed. Only one may survive. Believe it or not, we brought her to the Underland to protect her," said Vikus.

"And to protect yourselves," Gregor said flatly.

"Yes. And to protect ourselves," said Vikus. "But as our destinies are intertwined, it seemed one and the same thing. So, what will it be? Shall we take you home, or will you play out your hand with us?"

Gregor thought about the scraping sounds he sometimes heard in the walls of their apartment. They made his mom nervous even though his dad said it was probably just mice. But what if it was rats? And what if they were just a few inches of plaster away, watching Boots? Watching and waiting and reporting to the giant rats below.

There was a skittering sound at the door. Gregor looked over to see Boots riding in the door on the back of a giant roach with a bent antenna.

"Ge-go!" She giggled. "I ride! Temp take Boots ride!"

She was so happy . . . and tiny . . . and powerless . . . he couldn't watch her twenty-four hours a day . . . he had to go to school . . . there was no one else to protect her . . . even he had been worthless today . . . if it happened again, the rats could kill her in a New York minute. Not even.

"We're staying," said Gregor. "We're staying until this thing is over."

"Go, Ge-go!" Boots told Temp, tapping her heels on the roach's shell, and he obediently carried her over to Gregor. She slid off and ran over and hugged his leg.

"Hey, Boots," he said, ruffling her curls. "Where've you been?"

"I go ride! Fast! Fast ride!" she said.

"Do you remember Vikus?" Gregor asked, gesturing to him.

"Hi! Hi, you!" Boots said happily.

"Welcome, Boots," said Vikus. "We have missed you."

"Hi, bat!" Boots said, waving to Ares, although Gregor had been ignoring him.

"Hey, Temp," Gregor said to the cockroach. "Next

time, do you think you could tell me before you run off with Boots? You freaked me out."

"Hates us, the Overlander, hates us?" asked Temp.

Oh, great, now he'd hurt the roach's feelings. They were so thin-skinned. Well, thin-shelled. "No, I don't hate you, come on. It just scared me when you took Boots. I didn't know where she was," said Gregor.

"With us, she was, with us," said Temp, confused now.

"Yeah, I know that. Now. But I didn't know in the park," said Gregor. "I was worried."

"Hates us, the Overlander, hates us?" repeated Temp.

"No! I just need you to tell me if you're going to take her somewhere," said Gregor. Temp's antennas drooped noticeably. This was going nowhere fast. He shifted gears. "But, Temp? Thanks a lot for getting Boots away from the rats. You did a great job."

Temp perked up. "Rat bad," he said with conviction.

"Yeah," Gregor agreed. "Rat very bad."

At that moment, Luxa appeared in the doorway. Her silvery blond hair had grown out a little, she was a bit taller, but it was the lilac circles under those violet eyes that caught Gregor's attention. He wasn't the only one who'd been having a rough time lately.

"Welcome, Gregor the Overlander," said Luxa, approaching him but not touching him.

"Hey, Luxa, how you doing?" asked Gregor.

Her hand reached up distractedly and gave a quick nudge to the gold band around her head. Almost like she wanted to shove it off. "Fine, I am fine."

She wasn't fine. Clearly the girl hadn't been sleeping well. She did not look happy. But she still had that arrogant tilt to her head, that half smile. She still stood like a queen. "So, you have come back after all."

"Didn't have much choice," said Gregor.

"No," said Luxa stonily. "You and I never seem to have much choice. Arc you hungry?"

"I hungry. I hungry!" said Boots.

"We missed dinner," Gregor said, although his stomach was too knotted up to feel hungry.

"You need to bathe and dine and then sleep. Solovet says you must begin training on the morrow," said Luxa.

"Says she so?" Vikus asked, sounding a bit surprised.

"Yes. Did she not tell you?" said Luxa, giving Vikus a mocking look to which he did not respond. They had a funny relationship. Vikus was her grandfather but, since her parents had been killed by rats, he was also the closest thing she had to a father. And he was supervising and training Luxa to take on the full responsibilities of being the queen of Regalia when she reached sixteen. Gregor thought it must be complicated for them, being so many things to each other.

"I will see you on the field, Gregor, Ares," Luxa said, and left.

Gregor and Boots were taken to the bathrooms by a couple of Underlanders he'd never met. The young woman took Boots into the locker room for girls, while a guy escorted Gregor to his side.

He caused a scene by running out of the bathroom, dripping wet, with just a towel around him, to ask the guy not to burn their clothes. Ares was right, turning their clothes to ashes was standard, but Gregor knew it would cost a lot to replace them. And he really didn't want to lose his boots.

"But . . . your clothes carry much scent. The gnawers will know you are here," the guy said uncertainly.

"Oh, that's okay. I mean, they already know I'm here. Two of them chased me to the Waterway," said Gregor. "So, could you just . . . I don't know, maybe you could put them in the museum or something. That's all Overlander stuff, right?"

Relieved at the suggestion, the guy went off to ask Vikus.

They were fed a big meal: beef stew, bread, mushrooms, those things that reminded Gregor of sweet potatoes but weren't, and some kind of cake. Boots ate with gusto, which reminded him she'd had little more than a bowl of oatmeal and a peanut butter sandwich that day. At least the rest of his family would have the scalloped potatoes for dinner. If anyone could eat.

Oh, this whole thing was his fault! If only he'd kept an eye on Boots, the roaches never would have run off with her. But then, the rats could have reached her first. He guessed he ought to feel grateful to everybody here for rescuing her, and he did, on one level. But on another, he resented them for dragging him back into their troubled world. What was it Vikus had said? ". . . as our destinies are intertwined, blah, blah, blah, blah." He wanted no part of it, but here he was. Again.

Boots conked out the minute her head hit the pillow, but Gregor felt restless and anxious. He couldn't sleep thinking about his family, the threat to Boots, and the looming presence of some giant white rat out there somewhere, waiting for him. He finally gave up and decided to take a walk around the palace. It should be fine; he wasn't trying to escape or anything this time.

The doorways he passed seemed to lead to people's living quarters. The common rooms, like the High Hall or the dining rooms, were open. But on Gregor's floor, curtains blocked most of the rooms from view. Stone doors must not have been practical, and the only wooden door he'd ever seen in the Underland led to the room filled with Sandwich's prophecies.

Gregor had been walking about ten minutes when he heard voices coming from one of the rooms. They were somewhat muffled by the curtain, but still audible because the people were arguing. It was Vikus. . . .

"You should have told me about the training. I should have had a say in it!"

And who was he talking to?

"Yes, yes, we could have gone round and round while you tried to think of some way to protect him, but it is not possible. No matter what you want."

It sounded like Solovet. She was Vikus's wife, Luxa's grandmother, and the head of Regalia's military. Usually she spoke in a gentle, stately voice. But Gregor had heard her barking orders in combat. Solovet's ability to swing between gracious lady and soldier unnerved him because he never knew which one to expect. She sounded more like the soldier now.

Gregor didn't want to eavesdrop, so he turned to slip away. But then he heard his name and couldn't help listening.

"And what of what Gregor wants? Does he have no say in this? He pushed away the sword, Solovet. He does not wish to fight," said Vikus.

"None of us wish to fight, Vikus," said Solovet.

Vikus made a sound like "Hm," which suggested he thought maybe somebody in the room enjoyed fighting.

"None of us wish to fight," Solovet repeated in a steely voice, "but we all do. And the prophecy calls Gregor 'the warrior,' after all. Not 'the peacemaker.'"

"Oh, the prophecies are often misleading. He is called a warrior, but perhaps his weapons are not the ones we are familiar with. He did very well last time with no common weapon," said Vikus. "I am telling you he pushed away Sandwich's sword!"

"Yes, when he was safe and he thought everything was over. But I remember he asked for a sword on the quest," shot back Solovet.

"But he had no need of it. He was better off without it, I think," said Vikus.

"And I think that if you send him out unarmed this time, you guarantee his death," said Solovet.

Then there was silence.

Gregor retreated from the doorway as quickly as possible and somehow made it back to his room.

The little sleep he had that night was filled with disturbing dreams.

CHAPTER

6

The next morning Gregor was exhausted and in a bad mood. Another Underlander he'd never met served him breakfast. He left Boots under the care of the woman who'd bathed her the night before, and headed out. Today, he was supposed to start his training. Whatever that was.

After walking down a few halls, Gregor realized he had no idea where to go. Luxa had mentioned something about a field. Did she mean that sports arena? It was the first thing he had seen in Regalia, the large stone oval where the Underlanders played some kind of ball game on bats. It was a twenty-minute hike from the palace.

Gregor eventually made his way to an exit flanked by two guards. Outside the doorway was a platform attached by ropes. When he asked the guards if they would lower him to the ground, they reacted with surprise. "Did not your flier arrange to meet you in the High Hall to carry you to training?" said one.

Ares and Gregor had parted ways the previous night without exchanging a single word. "No, Ares must have forgotten," he said.

"Ah, yes, Ares," the guard said, and gave his partner a significant look.

Although Gregor was angry with Ares, he didn't like what it implied. "I forgot, too," he said. "I should have reminded him."

The guards nodded and made way for him to step onto the platform, which they then lowered the two hundred feet to the ground. Although the passage was smooth and uneventful, Gregor clutched the ropes tensely. The Underland provided endless opportunities to renew his fear of heights.

The city was bustling with pale-skinned, violet-eyed inhabitants going about their business. A lot of people stared at him, but if he caught their eye they gave him a respectful nod. A few even bowed. They knew him, or at least of him. He was the warrior who had saved their city from destruction. He actually enjoyed the attention for a while, and then he realized that they were probably thinking about how he had to go after that giant white rat. He wondered how many soldiers they would send with him to kill it. Something that big, that vicious . . . it might take a whole army!

When he arrived at the arena, it was clear that he was late. Groups of Underlanders of all ages were spread around the moss-covered ground doing various kinds of stretches and calisthenics. It didn't seem all that different from how they warmed up in track practice. As he looked around for Luxa, a voice caught his attention:

"Overlander! You are back!" And before he knew it, Mareth had him in a rib-crushing hug. The soldier was one of his favorite Underlanders.

"Hey, Mareth," he said. "How's it going?"

"Very well, now that you are here. Come, you are to do general training with me," Mareth said, pointing Gregor toward a bunch of kids his own age.

As they jogged across the field, they passed a group of children drilling with swords. None of them looked more than six years old. Apparently it was never too soon to start training for war in the Underland.

Gregor spotted Luxa and took a place near her.

They only had time for a nod before the class was back in session.

Mareth led them through a series of stretches. Gregor wasn't naturally limber. But Luxa could twist herself around like a pretzel.

Then there were some strengthening exercises, pretty standard push-ups, sit-ups, leg lifts. Finally, they ran laps around the arena. Gregor loved to run both sprints and distance. He felt satisfaction that he was the only one in his group able to keep pace with Mareth, who congratulated him at the end.

The glow from Mareth's praise quickly evaporated as they moved on to tumbling. They had gymnastics every year in gym class, and it was just something Gregor lived through until basketball started. He was too tall and lanky for it and seemed to end most moves by falling flat on his back. Which is what he did now.

Luxa stood over him, trying not to laugh. "When you roll, you cannot unbend your knees until your feet are on the ground," she said, offering him a hand up.

"Yeah, yeah, yeah," he said, letting her pull him up. Gymnasts were always giving you helpful tips like you could actually win the battle with gravity if you just concentrated hard enough.

Mareth called for her to demonstrate a trick, and off she went into some amazing run of twisty flippy things, landing on her feet as easily as Gregor would hop off a curb. The other Underlanders broke into spontaneous applause, and Luxa gave them one of her rare smiles. Then she came back and tried the hopeless task of teaching Gregor a cartwheel.

While she was explaining the mechanics for about the eighteenth time, "Hand, hand, foot, foot, not two hands then both feet," something caught her eye, and her face fell.

Gregor followed her gaze to the entrance of the arena, where a group of five kids was standing. He hadn't seen them before. "Who's that?"

"My cousins. They must have just arrived in Regalia," Luxa said stiffly.

Gregor looked at the group in surprise. "I thought your only cousins were Henry and, what's her name, the nervous girl?"

"Nerissa," said Luxa. "Yes, Nerissa and . . . Henry." The name cost her some effort to say. "They are the only royal cousins I have ever had. Our fathers were brothers, sons of a king, and of the royal family."

The cousins at the entrance spotted Luxa and began

to head over. She nodded at them with obvious dislike. "These five I am related to on my mother's side. They are not of royal blood, although they greatly desire to be so."

"Not crazy about them, huh?" said Gregor.

"They make fun of Nerissa. Of her gift and her frailty," said Luxa. "No, we do not . . . that is, I do not like them."

Gregor could tell that she and Henry had been "we" for so long that even months after his death she had trouble thinking of herself apart from him. This was, of course, complicated by the fact that he had utterly betrayed her to the rats in order to gain power himself. If you thought about it, it was no wonder Luxa had those lilac circles under her eyes.

"They are only here on a visit from the Fount. Hopefully it will be a short one," said Luxa.

Luxa and her cousins exchanged brief, formal greetings, and then she introduced Gregor to them. The oldest, Howard, was probably about sixteen and looked like he worked out a lot. There was a girl named Stellovet, maybe thirteen or so, who had flowing, silvery blond curls and was strikingly pretty. Next in line was a pair of younger twins, a girl named Hero and a boy called Kent. Lastly, there was a little girl, maybe five or so, clinging to Stellovet's hand. Her name sounded like the word "chimney," but he didn't think he'd gotten that right.

They had trouble taking their eyes off Gregor. He was probably the first Overlander they'd ever seen.

"Greetings, Gregor the Overlander. We have heard much of your deeds and are grateful for your return," Howard said, civilly enough.

"No problem," Gregor said, although his return was very problematic.

"Oh," said Stellovet, her voice dripping with honey, "we were so glad you were there to defend Luxa on the quest."

"Uh-huh. Well, I'd have been rat meat about three times if it wasn't for Luxa, so I guess it evens out," said Gregor.

Stellovet's eyes narrowed, but she gave him a sweet smile. "Yes, Luxa is something of an expert on rats. No matter how many legs they have."

It was a horrible thing to say. It was clear she meant Henry. Gregor knew kids like that, kids who would take something really awful in your life and use it against you. And there was nothing you could say about it because the thing was true. He felt a deep and instant dislike of Stellovet.

To his credit, Howard seemed embarrassed. Stellovet and the twins were smirking. The little girl, Chimney or whatever her name was, was wide-eyed and confused. Gregor didn't have to look at Luxa to know the pain that must be registering on her face.

Gregor stared at Stellovet for a moment and then said casually, "So, where are you guys from?"

"We live at the Fount. Our father is in charge there," Stellovet said with pride.

"You get a lot of rats at the Fount?" asked Gregor.

"Not many," said Stellovet. Now she was watching Gregor more closely. "They are no doubt afraid of our fighting abilities."

"They have little reason to come," Howard said, giving his sister a disapproving look. "They would have to swim their way up treacherous river rapids, and we have no crops or Overlanders worth destroying."

"Oh, so have you ever even seen a rat?" Gregor said pointedly to Stellovet.

She blushed, turning bright pink from head to toe. "Yes! I have seen a rat! On the riverbank! As close as I am to you!"

"But, Stellovet," said little Chimney, tugging on her hand, "that rat was dead."

Stellovet blushed an even deeper shade of pink. "Hush!" she said to Chimney angrily.

"That's about what I thought," said Gregor. "Hey, Luxa, weren't you going to show me that flip thing again?"

"If you will excuse us, cousins," Luxa said.

Luxa and Gregor turned and walked away. He caught her eye. The hurt was still evident on her face, but she gave him a smile. "Thank you, Gregor," she said softly.

"They're idiots," he answered with a shrug. "Go ahead, Luxa, do one of those flip things. Do the fanciest, wildest one you can think of."

Luxa paused for a moment, focused on a spot halfway across the field, and took off. She launched into a beautiful sequence of flips, ending with a move where she turned two full times in the air completely stretched out and landed on her feet. People applauded, but she just jogged back to Gregor as if she didn't notice. "Now you try," she said.

"Just give me some space," Gregor said, swinging his arms as if to loosen up, and she laughed.

Then Mareth called them all together to begin sword training. Howard and Stellovet had joined their group. Everyone chose a sword from a large cart that had been wheeled out onto the field. Gregor examined the weapons, unsure of what to do.

"Here, Overlander, try this one," said Mareth. He picked up a sword, resting the bottom of the blade against the back of his wrist, and offered Gregor the hilt.

Gregor's fingers closed around the handle, and he felt the weight of the sword in his hand, heavy at the hilt, light at the tip. He waved it a couple of times in the air, and it made a swishing sound.

"How does it feel?" asked Mareth.

"All right, I guess," said Gregor. It didn't feel like much of anything, really. He was sort of relieved. All that warrior stuff made him nervous. He didn't like fighting, and he was glad he didn't feel any different while holding the sword.

Mareth divided up the rest of the group into pairs to practice drills. Then he took Gregor aside for his first sword-fighting lesson. The soldier showed him different attacks you could make with the blade, and different ways to defend those attacks. Gregor didn't really see the point in this, since it seemed unlikely he'd be fighting a human, but he guessed this was just basic stuff that everybody had to learn.

After a while they broke to rest for a few minutes, and then Mareth announced it was time for cannon practice.

"Cannon practice? We're going to shoot off cannons?" Gregor asked Luxa.

"Oh, no, these are small cannons for sword practice. To help with speed and accuracy," said Luxa. "You will see."

Three small cannons were wheeled onto the field. Off to the side, Mareth set a barrel that was filled with waxy things about the size of a golf ball. "These are blood balls," Luxa said, holding one out on her palm.

When Gregor took it, he could feel some sort of liquid sloshing around inside it. "It's filled with blood?" he asked, kind of grossed out.

"No, only a red liquid to suggest blood. It makes it easier to see if one has made a hit or not," said Luxa.

The three cannons were positioned in an arc and loaded up with five blood balls each. The Underlanders gathered in a circle outside the cannons.

"So, who is brave enough to go first?" Mareth asked with a smile. "Why not you, Howard? I remember you did quite well the last time you visited."

Howard took his position between the cannons. One faced him, one was on his right, the last on his left. Each was about twenty feet away. On Mareth's command, three Underlanders started to crank handles on the sides of the cannons. Blood balls began to rocket out of the barrels straight at Howard. He swung his sword back and forth, trying to cover his front and sides. Seven blood balls burst as his blade made contact with them. But another eight lay unharmed on the ground around him. The whole thing only took about ten seconds.

"Well done, Howard! Well done," said Mareth, and Howard looked pleased with himself.

"Was that good?" Gregor asked Luxa.

She shrugged. "It was not bad" was as much praise as she could muster.

One by one, each of the students took their turn in the line of fire. Some hit only one or two balls. Luxa matched Howard's seven, and Stellovet hit a respectable five. When all the Underlanders had gone, Mareth called for the cannons to be moved to another part of the field.

"Does not the Overlander take a turn?" Stellovet asked in an innocent voice.

"This is his first day of sword practice," said Mareth.

"I suppose it is too daunting," said Stellovet, "even for one so accomplished."

"I greatly doubt Gregor is daunted," Mareth said with respect. "But our weapons are unfamiliar to him. Would you like to try it, Gregor? Only as an exercise. Almost no one gets many on their first try."

"Sure, why not?" said Gregor. It was funny; he *did* sort of want to. He had a feeling it was like those county fairs he'd been to in Virginia, though. They had these games like tossing a softball into an old milk jug, or getting a quarter to land on a glass plate. They looked simple, but when you tried them, they were next to impossible. Still, you had to try.

Gregor took his place between the cannons. He held his sword out in front of him like he'd seen the Underlanders do. He felt that slightly anxious, slightly excited feeling he had when it was his turn to bat in baseball. He heard Mareth give the order to fire.

And then a strange thing happened. As the first ball left the cannon in front of him, the arena, the Underlanders, almost everything around him seemed to mute and grow indistinct. He was aware only of the blood balls flying toward him from all directions. His arm was moving. He could hear his blade making a whistling sound. Something splattered against his face. And then it was over.

His surroundings came back into focus: first the walls of the arena, then the shocked faces of the Underlanders. He could feel liquid dripping off his face and hands. The pounding of his heart was audible. He looked down at the ground.

At his feet lay the oozing shells of fifteen balls.

CHAPTER

7

Gregor opened his fingers, and the sword fell to the ground. It was shiny with the red liquid, which, if it wasn't actually blood, sure looked like it. He ran his sword hand across the front of his shirt, leaving a big red stain. Suddenly he felt sick.

He turned on his heel and walked away from the sword, from the blood balls, from the Underlanders who were now beginning to talk in excited voices. Word of what he'd just done must have been spreading around the arena, because people were rushing toward the cannon area. He could feel them beginning to press in on him, and someone, Mareth maybe, called his name. It was becoming hard to breathe.

Suddenly Ares was there before him. "I know a place" was all he said.

Gregor automatically climbed on his back, and they took off. He could hear several people calling for him as they flew out of the stadium, but Ares didn't stop. They headed not in the direction of Regalia, but into the tunnels opposite the entrance to the city.

"You will want light," Ares said, angling in toward a row of torches on the tunnel wall, and Gregor reached out and snagged one. In the torchlight, his hand glistened wet and red. He looked away.

Ares dove off into a side tunnel that forked repeatedly. Eventually they arrived at a small underground lake flanked by dozens of caves. The bat dove into one with a narrow entrance. Inside, the cave opened up into a wide space. Large crystal formations grew down from the high ceiling. Gregor slid off Ares's back and onto the stone floor.

He pressed his forehead into his knees and let his breathing return to normal. What had happened back there? How had he hit all fifteen blood balls? He'd been running sword drills with Mareth and nothing unusual had happened, but when those blood balls had started flying at him . . .

"Did you see? Did you see what I did?" he asked

Ares. He had seen some bats flying around the arena that morning, but he hadn't noticed Ares.

The bat sat motionless for a moment, then answered. "You broke all the blood balls."

"I hit them all," Gregor said, still trying to remember it. "But I don't even know how to use a sword."

"Apparently you learn quickly," said Ares, and somehow that made Gregor laugh a little. He looked around the cave. There were food supplies, blankets, spare torches.

"What's this place? Like, your hideout?" Gregor asked.

"Yes, my hideout," said Ares. "At one time it was also Henry's. We came here when we did not want to be around others. Now it is less my hideout than my home."

The implication of what the bat was saying began to dawn on Gregor. "So, you don't live with the other bats anymore? I thought when I bonded with you it made things okay again — about Henry and all."

"It spared me from official banishment. But no one save Aurora and Luxa will speak to me," said Ares.

"Not even Vikus?" Gregor asked, forgetting his own problems for a minute.

"Well, yes, Vikus. But he will speak to anyone," Ares said without much enthusiasm.

He had had no idea things were so bad for the bat. If he hadn't been banished physically, he had been banished socially from his world. And then when Gregor had shown up again, all he'd done was order him around. "Look, I really am sorry about yesterday," he said. "I was mad and scared about Boots, and I took it out on you."

"I was angry, too, about many things that have little to do with you," said Ares.

So, it was better between them. But Gregor still felt like Ares was a stranger.

"How'd you hook up with Henry, anyway?" he blurted out. Maybe it wasn't polite to ask, but it was the main thing Gregor wanted to know.

"Henry chose me because I was wild and known to disobey many of the rules of my land. I chose Henry because I was flattered and he was royal and under his protection I knew I could be absolved of many things," said Ares. "It was not all bad. We flew well together and shared many of the same tastes. In most ways, we were suited to each other. In one, we were not."

So among bats Ares had been some bad-boy rebel type. Of course, that was the kind of bat Henry would pick. Gregor had picked Ares, too, because the bat had risked everything to save his life — but would he have chosen him if the circumstances hadn't been so extraordinary? He didn't know.

There was a rustling of wings at the cave entrance, and Aurora flew in with Luxa.

"We knew you would be here!" cried Luxa. She bounced off Aurora and almost danced across the floor, clapping her hands together. "Was it not wonderful? Did you see it? Did you see the look on Stellovet's face?"

"As if she had a mouth full of vinegar," Aurora purred, apparently also in a good mood.

"Why?" said Gregor.

"Why? Because of you and the blood balls!" Luxa said, as if he were dense. "She thought to make you look like a fool, and instead you hit the total! Almost no one has ever done this, Gregor! It was brilliant!"

For the first time, Gregor felt a tinge of pride in his accomplishment. Maybe he had overreacted, because of the fake blood and all. Maybe he'd actually just done a really cool thing, like running the table in pool, or pitching a no-hitter in baseball. "Yeah?" he said.

"Of course! And I have not seen Stellovet so put out since the picnic!" said Luxa, giggling at the memory.

The bats both began to make a "huh, huh, huh" sound, and it took a moment for Gregor to realize they were laughing.

"Oh, Gregor, you should have seen it. Vikus forced us all to go on this picnic with my Fount cousins because he thought it would help us get along better. And Stellovet kept pretending she heard rats, and making Nerissa terrified. So Henry tricked her into eating moth cocoons. She spent the whole afternoon picking silk out of her teeth and saying, 'Ah will noth forgeth thiseth!'" Luxa said, doing a pretty great imitation of someone with their mouth full of silk.

"How'd he get her to eat cocoons?" Gregor asked, both amused and grossed out.

"He told her they were a delicacy reserved only for royalty and he could not offer her any. So of course she stole a handful and stuffed it in her mouth," said Luxa.

"Henry could trick her into anything," Ares said, followed by a few more "huh, huh, huhs." And then suddenly his laughter faded. "He could trick all of us."

A cloud seemed to fall on the bats and Luxa. Henry had treated them far worse than he had treated Stellovet.

"Whatever Henry was wrong about, he was right about my Fount cousins," Luxa said grimly. "Especially Stellovet. She dreams of Nerissa and me dying because she thinks Vikus would be made king then and she, as his granddaughter, would be a princess."

They were all quiet for a time, then Aurora piped up on a more positive note. "Gregor's feat will be good for you, Ares."

"We shall see," said Ares.

"It will. It will do you no harm to have a bond who can hit the total," said Luxa. "No one will dare ignore you now."

Gregor hoped this was true. It didn't seem like Ares had much of a life.

Suddenly Ares's and Aurora's heads shot up. Luxa listened a second and then leaped onto Aurora's back. They were gone in a flash.

Gregor could hear some kind of horn blowing in the distance. It had a high, wailing pitch. "What is it?"

"It is a warning, Overlander. You had best mount up," said Ares.

Gregor grabbed a torch and threw his leg over Ares's neck. They were immediately airborne.

"Warning? What kind of a warning?" he asked as they swerved out over the lake.

Ares spoke calmly, but his muscles were tense. "It means that rats have entered Regalia."

CHAPTER

8

G regor gripped Ares's fur and immediately assumed the worst. If rats were in Regalia, they must have come for one thing: Boots!

"Hurry, Ares! Please!" said Gregor.

"Yes, Overlander, I will hurry," said Ares. His powerful wings were beating up and down in a blur. "And Luxa and Aurora will go straight to your sister."

It was only a few minutes, but it seemed to take forever to get back to the arena. Gregor had visions of an army of rats ripping their way across Regalia with one target in mind. Maybe the giant white rat itself had come to kill her!

As they sped into the stadium, a guard shouted at them and waved at the massive stone doors that separated the playing field from the city. "There are just the two! There, by the doors! Stay back!"

Ares put on the brakes, but they were close enough to get a good view of the battle on the ground. In front of the doors were two rats fighting for their lives against a dozen humans on bats. The smaller rat seemed to be able to leap amazingly high off the ground. It was not getting a lot of action, though, because a much larger rat was shielding it from the brunt of the attack.

The big rat was moving so quickly that Gregor couldn't tell much about it. It was spinning in a circle, springing from its front feet to its back feet, lashing out at anything that came within reach of its claws and teeth. He could see bats and humans getting wounded, but not a single blow was landing on the rat. It was like watching one of those martial arts movies where no one can touch the main sensei or master or whatever, it was like watching —

"Oh, no!" Gregor exclaimed. "It's him. It's got to be —"

"Ripred!" Ares cut him off.

"Stop them!" said Gregor.

Ares was already diving. He swooped in from the

side, knocking two riders off the front line. He did a figure eight that disoriented a few more, and did some strange hovering motion in the air over Ripred's head.

"Stop!" yelled Gregor. "Stop, he's a friend!"

The Underlanders pulled back to avoid hitting him, and began to shout angrily at Ares to move.

"No, you don't understand! He's on our side! It's Ripred!" Gregor hollered over the din. They heard the name Ripred, and the Underlanders pulled back in silence.

The big rat stopped spinning and fell almost lazily on its back. Its scarred face broke into a big, fanged grin, and it started to laugh. "Oh, look at them, Overlander. Are they not priceless?"

Gregor wanted to laugh, too, because some of the Underlanders' mouths were literally hanging open, but he stifled the impulse. "Stop it," he said to Ripred. "It's not funny."

Ripred just guffawed even louder. "You know it is! You know you want to laugh, too!"

It was such a silly thing to say in the midst of all the tension that it caught Gregor off guard, and he did kind of laugh. He stopped himself quickly, but it was too late. Everyone had heard him. "Just shut up, okay?" he said to Ripred, who ignored him completely as he chortled in glee.

"Can somebody get, like, Vikus, or Solovet, or somebody?" Gregor asked. None of the Underlanders answered him or flew off. He noticed the smaller rat hunkered back against the doors, wide-eyed and panting. He figured it was a friend of Ripred's. "Hey, sorry about this. I'm Gregor. Nice to meet you."

The rat pulled its gums back from its teeth and hissed viciously at him, causing both Gregor and Ares to flinch.

Ripred was beating his tail on the ground in a spasm of hilarity. "Oh! Oh! You needn't try to sweet-talk her," he gasped. "Twitchtip hates everybody!"

The smaller rat, Twitchtip, snarled at Ripred. Then she tore a hole in the moss with one slash of her paw and buried her nose in it.

Okay, well, she was weird.

"Ground formation," commanded a voice, and Gregor turned to see Solovet on a bat coming in for a landing. The Underlanders brought their bats down in a tight diamond pattern. Ignoring Ripred, Solovet walked through the soldiers and bats, sending the wounded off to get medical attention. Then she dismissed the rest.

By this time, Ripred had pulled himself together and was stretched out comfortably on his side. Twitchtip still had her nose buried in the hole in the moss. She was breathing through her mouth in short, distressed puffs.

Solovet crossed to the rats, signaling Ares to land as she went. She surveyed the invaders stonily. "I have just sent eleven of my ranks to the hospital."

"Oh, I barely scratched them. I was just giving them a little live rat practice, and I think we both have to admit they need it," Ripred said with a significant nod.

"You were supposed to meet an escort guard at Queenshead tomorrow," said Solovet.

"Was that tomorrow? I felt certain it was today. And we waited and waited and poor Twitchtip was so eager for her first glimpse of Regalia that I didn't have the heart to disappoint her another minute. Right, Twitchtip?" Ripred said, poking the rat with the tip of his tail.

Twitchtip yanked her nose from the moss, snapped at Ripred's tail, which he whipped out of reach just in time, and shoved her nose back in the earth.

"Isn't she a charmer? Isn't she just irresistible?" said Ripred. "And I've had her all to myself on a journey from the Dead Land. Imagine the fun."

Twitchtip glowered at him but didn't attack again.

"And for what reason do we have the pleasure of her company?" Solovet asked, eyeing Twitchtip.

"Why, I brought her as a gift. For you, for your people, and for Gregor here. Yes, especially for Gregor," said Ripred.

Gregor looked at the seething rat with alarm. "For me? She's a gift for me?"

"Well, not literally. It's not as if I own her. But I made a bargain with her. She's agreed to help you find the Bane, and I've agreed to let her live with my merry little band of rats in the Dead Land if she succeeds," said Ripred. "You see, she was driven out of the gnawers' land years ago and has been surviving on her own."

"Because she is mad," Solovet said, as if that were obvious.

"Oh, no, not mad. Twitchtip is gifted. Show the people what you can do, Twitchtip," said Ripred. Twitchtip just glared at him. "Go on, show them, or it's back to living with me, myself, and I for you."

Twitchtip reluctantly lifted up her head and brushed the moss and dirt from her nose. She tilted back her chin, took a deep sniff, and grimaced. "The boy's sister is located on the third level of a large circular structure in a room with eight other pups and two grown ones. She's just eaten cake and milk. She's cutting a new tooth. Her catch cloth is wet, and her shirt is pink," Twitchtip spat out. Then she crammed her nose back in the moss.

Solovet's eyebrows shot up. "She is a scent seer?"

"Yes, her sense of smell is so unnaturally heightened she can even detect color. She is one in a million. An anomaly. A fluke. A pariah because her own species finds her gift so disquieting. But very, very useful, I think, to you, my dear Solovet," said Ripred.

"She is not a bad fighter, either. If she has survived alone in the Dead Land." For the first time, Solovet smiled. "Can you stay to dine, Ripred?"

"I can be persuaded," said Ripred. "Have them make the thing with the shrimp, won't you? And no skimping on the cream."

"No skimping on the cream," agreed Solovet.

"And give Twitchtip plenty of food, but make it bland. Handle it as little as possible. Your scent is repulsive to her," said Ripred.

Solovet gave orders for Twitchtip to be taken to a remote cave outside Regalia, where the city's smells wouldn't be so torturous to her.

Before they left, Solovet turned to Gregor. "I have not had time to welcome you properly, Gregor. I hear you made quite a stir at training today."

"I guess," said Gregor.

"He hit the total," Solovet said to Ripred.

"Did he?" Ripred said, surveying him with interest. Suddenly Ripred's tail came up out of nowhere and sliced at Gregor. To Gregor's surprise, he found the rat's tail clenched in his hand. He had reflexively blocked it inches from his face.

"Well, you can't teach that," Ripred said, slipping his tail out of Gregor's grasp.

Ripred went off to the palace with Solovet through some secret passage to avoid causing a panic in the city.

Ares flew Gregor back to the palace. Guards greeted him at the High Hall and, after a moment of discomfort, they greeted Ares as well. Maybe Aurora was right. Maybe things would be better for the bat now that he was bonded to someone who could hit a lot of blood balls.

In the bath, he scrubbed and scrubbed at the fake

blood, but it still left a stain on his skin. He finally gave up, hoping it would wear off before he went back to school — after the white rat was dead or whatever.

He went to get Boots from the nursery and was happy to see Dulcet, the really nice nanny who had cared for the toddler the first trip down. "How's she been doing?"

"Oh, Boots has had a very good day. I think it has been somewhat trying for Temp, though," said Dulcet, nodding toward a corner.

For the first time, Gregor spotted the giant cockroach. He was being decked out in dress-up clothes by a group of little kids. Each of his insect legs wore a different kind of shoe. His head poked out of a long purple gown that bunched up around his neck. Pink ribbons festooned his drooping antennas. Boots plunked a fuzzy hat on his head, and the kids all jumped up and down, squealing in delight.

"Temp have hat! Temp have hat!" she beamed at Gregor as he came to get her.

"Ohhh," Temp said mournfully. "Ohhh."

"He sure does," said Gregor. "He looks real good, too. But now it's time for dinner, Boots." He knelt down and whispered to Temp, "Don't worry, buddy.

I'll get you out of here." Trying not to laugh, he began to untangle the poor insect from the clothes. He'd been the object of Boots's dress-up games often enough to feel sympathetic. This had probably been going on for hours.

Unhappily, dinner turned out to be a reunion of sorts for those who had gone on "The Prophecy of Gray" quest — those who had survived it, anyway. Of the eight who had lived to tell the tale, only Gregor's dad was absent. Gregor, Boots, Luxa, Aurora, Ares, Temp, and Ripred were all there, with Solovet and Vikus presiding over the table. Maybe Vikus had thought this would give them some kind of comfort, but if the memories it brought up of the dead — the two spiders, Gox and Treflex, the cockroach, Tick, and Luxa's cousin, Henry — were painful for Gregor, they had to be excruciating for some of the other survivors.

It didn't help that this was the first time Boots seemed to notice that Tick was gone. Boots had been asleep with a high fever when Tick had given her life to protect her. When they'd gotten back home, Boots had talked about Tick as if she were fine. Gregor let her because he didn't know how to explain to a two-year-old that her friend was dead and, besides, he'd never planned on coming back here, anyway. Now her little voice going, "Where Tick? Where Tick?" sent jolts of sadness through him.

After several minutes of "Where Tick?" almost everyone had given up eating. Without even excusing himself, Ares just up and flew out of the room, and Temp hid under the table, making odd clicking noises that Gregor thought might be some kind of cockroach crying.

Even Ripred seemed to raise an eyebrow at the guest list. "Really, Vikus, did you think we were going to swap war stories?"

"I thought it might be healing," said Vikus. "That it might help some accept their losses."

At that, Luxa sprang up, kicking her chair back onto the floor behind her. She and Aurora were gone in seconds.

"And it's working beautifully," said Ripred. "Ah, well, more for me." The rat hooked his paw around a huge serving dish of shrimp in cream sauce and pulled it in front of him. He stuck his entire face in the dish and sucked it down. At least this distracted Boots, who was so fascinated by his eating methods that she dipped her own face in her plate to imitate him.

"Mm," Ripred said dreamily as he pulled his dripping muzzle from the dish.

"Mm," Boots echoed. She giggled, dropped her face back in her dish, and slurped.

Ripred's long tongue swept around his jaws, cleaning off the cream. "Nothing like that in the Dead Land. Nothing much of anything these days, of course. Since the humans have cut the gnawers off from their main fishing grounds."

"Perhaps a little hunger will help them reflect on their poor judgment in attacking us," Solovet said, helping herself to a large serving of mushrooms.

"Surely the gnawers are not really starving?" asked Vikus.

"Aren't they?" said Ripred. "You have driven them back to the border of the ants. The rivers left open to them are dangerous to fish and are downstream from the crawlers, so the catch is small. What, in your mind, are they feeding on?"

There was silence.

Gregor tried to imagine being a rat and being hungry. In his experience, being hungry didn't make you think about anything but getting food — or maybe, in the rats' case, getting even.

"It's not helping the grand plan. I have enough to overcome as it is. And you reap what you sow, Solovet," said Ripred.

"Is this what you came to tell me, Ripred?" Solovet said, unmoved.

"No. You know what you're doing. Or at least you flatter yourself you do. I came to deliver Twitchtip and to teach Gregor another trick he can't learn from you." Ripred stuck an entire loaf of bread in his mouth and pushed back from the table. "Ready, boy?"

"For what?" Gregor asked, watching the crumbs fly out of Ripred's mouth.

"Your first lesson," Ripred said with a big gulp. "It starts now."

"Echolocation?" Gregor said blankly. "You're going to teach me echolocation?" He was standing in a circular cave somewhere deep beneath Regalia with nothing but his mini flashlight.

Ripred slouched against a wall. Even for a rat, he had terrible posture. When he fought, everything in his body seemed to align and crackle with energy and power. The rest of the time, he wasn't much to look at. He reminded Gregor of one of those big base-ball pitchers who kind of lumber around with their stomachs almost popping off their uniform buttons. You wouldn't bet they could make it around the bases without having to stop and catch their breath. But put them on the pitcher's mound and they'd fire off a hundred-mile-an-hour fastball that left the batter cross-eyed.

As if even slouching had been too much of an effort for him, Ripred slid down and lounged along the wall of the cave. "Yes, echolocation. Tell me what you know about it."

"I know bats use it. And dolphins, maybe. It's like radar. They make a sound and it bounces off of something and they can tell where it is without seeing it," said Gregor. "But people can't do that. I can't do that."

"Anybody can do it, to some extent. In the Overland, some blind people use it with excellent results," said Ripred. "The Underland humans don't give it much attention, but in this, they are fools. All the rest of us down here use it to some degree."

"You mean, the roaches and the spiders and —" started Gregor.

"All of us. Generations in the dark have helped the skill evolve. But if you could master even the most rudimentary elements of it, echolocation would be invaluable to you," said Ripred. "Say, for instance, if you lost your light in a cave with a rat."

Gregor saw Ripred's tail coming, and his hand lifted to block it, but the rat was ahead of him this time. It was actually his hind foot that smacked the flashlight out of Gregor's hand and sent it spinning into the cave wall twenty feet away. The beam pointed into the stone, leaving them virtually in the dark.

Ripred's voice startled him. "And now I'm back here," the rat said from behind him. Gregor whipped around and, from somewhere off to his left, Ripred whispered, "Over here now."

The flashlight came spinning back across the floor and bumped into Gregor's feet. He picked it up and saw the rat was again slouching against the wall, on the far side of the cave from where the flashlight had been.

"So teach me," Gregor said, unnerved.

Ripred began by having him close his eyes and make a clicking sound, bouncing his tongue off the roof of his mouth. Then he had to listen very carefully to how it sounded. It was supposed to sound differently when he directed it toward a cave wall than when he directed it at Ripred. Then Ripred had him turn off his flashlight and click and listen and point it wherever it sounded like the rat might be.

He really did try, but he'd only had about three hours of sleep in the last two days, plus all the craziness of being back in the Underland and the prophecy and the training and —

"Focus, Overlander! This could save your life!" Ripred snarled as Gregor miscalculated his position for the tenth time in a row.

"This is stupid, Ripred — it all sounds the same to me!" Gregor snapped back. "I can't do it, okay?"

"No, not okay. You will practice. Every time you get a chance down here and when you go home, if you get home, whenever you can," ordered Ripred. "You may not master it, but clearly you can only improve!"

"Okay. Fine. I'll practice. Are we done?" Gregor asked with some attitude. He'd about had it with the rat.

Suddenly Ripred's nose was inches from his own. The rat's eyes were narrowed in anger.

"Listen, Warrior," he hissed. "One day you will find that it matters not if you can hit three thousand blood balls if you cannot locate one in the dark. Understand?"

"Yeah," Gregor managed to get out. Ripred didn't move. "So, I'll practice. I will," said Gregor. "For real."

"Good. Now let's go get some sleep. We're both done in," said Ripred.

As they silently made their way back toward the city, Gregor wondered if Ripred would think twice about killing him. When they had been on the quest to get his dad, Ripred had kept him alive because they had mutual need: Gregor needed Ripred to find his dad. Ripred needed Gregor to help defeat King Gorger so that he could be the leader of the rats someday. Ripred must still need Gregor for "The Prophecy of Bane." But when Gregor had stopped being of use to the rat, would he be expendable?

Gregor's feet dragged as he climbed up the flights of stairs toward where he thought his bedroom was. It was very late here — probably about the time he'd come into the city the previous night — and everyone was asleep. He got lost and couldn't find anyone to give him directions. As he was wandering around, looking for a guard, he came upon the wooden door that shut off the room filled with Sandwich's prophecies.

The door was cracked open. This was strange; he thought they kept it locked all the time. Someone must be inside.

He pushed the door open wider and stepped in. "Hello? Anybody in here?"

At first he thought the room was empty. The lamp was still lit under "The Prophecy of Bane," but no one appeared to be reading it. Then he heard a faint rustling sound in the far corner, and she stepped into the light.

"Oh!" Gregor jumped, not just because he was startled but because the sight of her was spooky. He had only seen Nerissa once. She had been saying goodbye to her brother, Henry, as they left on the quest. He remembered she was very thin and seemed nervous. She had given him a copy of "The Prophecy of Gray" to take on his journey. Luxa had told him she could see the future or something.

If she had been thin before, she was now emaciated. Her eyes shone huge and hollow in the torchlight. Where Luxa had lilac circles under her eyes, Nerissa's were underscored with dark purple crescents. Her hair, which fell down far below her waist, was loose and tangled. Even though she was wrapped in a thick cloak, she acted like she was freezing.

"Oh, I'm sorry. Didn't mean to — I'm just — I was just looking for sleeping — I mean, looking for where

I sleep. My bedroom. Sorry." Gregor started to back out of the room.

"No, wait, Overlander," Nerissa said in a tremulous voice. "Stay a moment."

"Oh, okay, sure," Gregor said, wishing very badly he could get out of there. "So, how've you been, Nerissa?" he said, and then cringed. How did he think she'd been?

"I have been unwell," Nerissa said tiredly. But it was not self-pitying, which somehow made it sadder.

"Look, I'm sorry about your brother, about Henry," said Gregor.

"I think it is best he is dead," said Nerissa.

"You do?" Gregor said, taken aback by her bluntness.

"When one considers the alternatives," said Nerissa. "Had he been successful in banding with the gnawers, we would all be dead. You, your sister, your father. All of my people. Henry, too. But, of course, I miss him greatly."

Well, she might be a wreck, but Nerissa was not afraid to look things in the eye. "Do you know why he did it?" Gregor ventured to ask.

"He was afraid. I know that. And I think somehow

in his mind he felt that joining with the rats would give him the security he longed for," said Nerissa.

"He was wrong," said Gregor.

"Was he?" Nerissa said, and she smiled. Which was extra spooky.

"I thought so. Didn't you just say . . . if he'd got his way, we'd all be dead?" said Gregor. Maybe she was kind of crazy, after all.

"Oh, yes. His methods were undoubtedly flawed." Nerissa lost interest in their conversation and wandered over to "The Prophecy of Bane." Her bony fingers reached up and ran slowly across the letters, as if she were reading Braille. "And what of you, Warrior? Are you ready to face the Bane?"

The Bane. Ripred had said something about the Bane. "You mean . . . the prophecy?" Gregor asked, confused.

"Vikus did not tell you? We call the white rat 'the Bane,'" said Nerissa. "Do you know what that means?"

"Not exactly," Gregor admitted.

"It means a scourge," said Nerissa.

Wow, that was helpful. A scourge. "Still not clear," said Gregor.

"A calamity, an affliction." Nerissa searched his face for signs of understanding. "A very bad thing," she said finally.

"Oh, I got you," said Gregor. "Well, yeah, the rat. Vikus says I'm a threat to it or something. I'm supposed to help you guys kill it."

Nerissa looked bewildered. "Help us? Oh, no, Gregor, you must drain its light. See, it is written here." Her fingers rapidly passed over a line on the wall.

WILL THE WARRIOR DRAIN YOUR LIGHT?

When Vikus had gone over the prophecy the night before, Gregor had been so consumed with the rats wanting to kill Boots, he hadn't focused much on this line. And Vikus hadn't elaborated. For the Underlanders, the word "light" was interchangeable with the word "life." So, when they talked about draining something's light, they meant killing it. The mission was to kill the Bane. He knew that. But Gregor had assumed the Underlanders would send a lot of soldiers with him. Trained soldiers.

The line pounded into his brain.

Gregor began to get a very bad feeling. "Oh, man," he said. "You mean, there's this giant white rat . . . and you guys expect me to . . . by myself . . . you mean, I'm supposed to . . ."

"Kill it, Gregor," said Nerissa. "The Bane must die by your hand alone."

PART 2

The Hunt

CHAPTER
10

Maybe you didn't actually have to have sleep. Maybe it was something people got used to having, and thought they needed, but could really get by without. Gregor hoped so, because despite his complete state of exhaustion, he'd just spent the night without a wink of it.

Mostly he'd been trying to imagine the big white rat he was supposed to kill by himself. A rat much larger and, presumably, stronger than Ripred. So Gregor figured the Bane was at least twice as tall as he was and probably weighed, oh, nine or ten times as much. Who cared if Gregor could hit a bunch of blood balls? This thing would squash him like a fly.

Of course, Vikus hadn't gone into any detail about it. The same way he had never really spent much time dwelling on the fact that four of the twelve questers would be dead when "The Prophecy of Gray" was fulfilled. He had a way of sidestepping issues he thought Gregor couldn't handle. How long would Vikus have put off telling him he had to kill the Bane alone? As long as possible. Gregor pictured himself gaping in terror at the salivating white giant while Vikus tapped him on the shoulder and said in an upbeat voice, "Oh, yes, and by the way, according to Sandwich, you have to kill him single-handedly. Off you go, then!"

Gregor remembered when he was standing in Central Park, barely over a day ago, and how his biggest worry had been how they were going to afford Christmas presents. Nothing like one of Sandwich's prophecies to put your whole world in perspective.

He shifted his chin to his other hand and tried to focus on the babble of voices around the stone table. Vikus had called a council meeting to discuss his journey to find and kill the Bane. The council was a group of older Underlanders who would govern Regalia by committee until Luxa turned sixteen and was of age to rule.

The only thing the members agreed on was that Gregor needed to get moving as soon as possible. Since the rats knew that Gregor and Boots were in the Underland again, they would surely take extra measures to conceal the Bane and hunt down his sister.

Apparently Regalian spies also had brand-new information and had just locked in on an area where they thought the white rat was hiding. Although none of them had personally seen the creature, their sources indicated it was in a place called the Labyrinth. The word meant nothing to Gregor, but Ares whispered to him that a labyrinth was a maze. Lizzie and her puzzle book flashed before his eyes. She would be so much better than he would at finding her way around a maze. Thinking of Lizzie made him think of the rest of his family waiting and wondering above, and the thought was unbearable.

"Yeah, let's get going. The sooner the better!" Gregor said, and everyone looked at him in surprise since it was the first thing he'd said all morning and the council was currently talking about which way to travel to the Labyrinth.

Although they examined several options, every route that went through the web of Underland tunnels was judged too dangerous. While the humans controlled a much wider range of the Underland than they had before the war, the Labyrinth was situated in a remote corner of the rats' land. So remote, in fact, that most rats never even went there. But if they had the Bane there, it was sure to be guarded.

"That leaves the Waterway," Vikus said with a frown. "It is not ideal, but it is the least treacherous."

"What of the serpents? Their mating season is nigh," said Howard. Gregor didn't know why Luxa's cousin had been allowed in the meeting. He was just supposed to be on a family visit.

"A good point," agreed Vikus. "And yet another reason to begin the journey at once. Perhaps the party can slip by before the serpents awaken."

"Yippee, serpents," Gregor thought, and he remembered a twenty-foot spiked tail he'd seen flipping out of the Waterway when Ares was flying them home. He wondered what was attached to the tail.

"Now, Gregor, there is something we need to address," said Vikus. "It is the opinion of the council that Boots should remain under guard in Regalia while you pursue the Bane."

Gregor had anticipated this coming up. It would be terribly dangerous taking Boots on another Underland trip. But how could he leave her here when he had seen

Ripred and Twitchtip get into the arena so easily? Sure, Ripred was extra smart, but none of the rats seemed dumb. He and Boots would stay together, like his mom always told them to do.

"She's coming with me or I don't go. End of discussion," said Gregor. He knew this sounded uppity, but at this point he was too tired to care.

There was a pause in which everyone glanced around, acknowledging that this had been out of line. But what were they going to do?

Vikus sent him off to prepare for the journey. He went to the museum to look for some light sources. The museum was full of stuff that had fallen from Gregor's world. There were a lot of cool, really old things, like a wheel from a horse-drawn carriage, an actual quiver still filled with arrows, a silver mug, a cuckoo clock, a top hat. More recent items, like wallets, jewelry, and watches, were neatly laid out in rows. There were lots of good flashlights, probably because anyone who had been in the tunnels below New York City would have needed one. Gregor selected four and dug out a lot of batteries.

A couple of life jackets caught his eye, and he took these, too. The last time, they had been traveling through stone tunnels. This time, he guessed they would be flying over the Waterway. Boots was too little to know how to swim. He added to his supplies a roll of duct tape and a couple of candy bars that didn't seem too stale.

As he was leaving, he saw their regular clothes folded in two neat stacks by the door. Vikus must've said it was okay to keep them. Gregor didn't care what they smelled like; he was wearing his boots.

When he went by the nursery to collect Boots, he was told that Dulcet had already taken her down to the river. That was to be their departure point.

Gregor thought that made sense, since flying down the river had to be the quickest way to get to the Waterway. But when he reached the docks, he saw a team of Underlanders loading up two boats that were suspended by ropes at dock level above the river. They were long, narrow vessels that reminded him of boats he'd seen in the museum back home, boats Native Americans had used hundreds of years ago. But secured to the bottom of each was a large gray triangular fin — a real fish fin — that must've come off a whopper of a swordfish or something. Strapped along the sides of the boats were more fins that could be extended and retracted horizontally as needed. A curved bone was attached to the back of each boat as a rudder.

"What's with the boats?" he asked Vikus, who was overseeing the loading. "Aren't we taking the bats?"

"Ah, yes, but the Waterway is vast and provides few hospitable places to rest. No bat would have the stamina to cross it, so much of your trip must be by sea," said Vikus.

Gregor didn't know much about boating except that, compared to flying, it was slow. It was going to take forever to get to the Bane by water.

Just then, Twitchtip slunk out onto the dock. "Oh, great," thought Gregor. "I bet I end up riding with the crazy rat."

Dulcet helped him secure the life jacket on Boots. It was too big, really, but they belted it on as best they could. Gregor wasn't sure what to do with the second jacket — he could swim pretty well — until he saw Temp shivering at the edge of the dock, looking at the churning river below.

"Hey, Temp, are you going with us?" he asked.

"Vikus says I may, he says," said Temp. So Gregor put the extra jacket on Temp. The bug allowed it because the princess was wearing one, too, and because Gregor got through to him that it would help him float.

As he stood up from strapping Temp in, he saw Luxa, Solovet, Mareth, and Howard come out of the palace. Luxa and Solovet were wearing gowns, not the long pants they had traveled in before.

"Wait a minute — you're going with us, right?" Gregor said to Luxa.

"No, Gregor, I cannot. I was only allowed to join you on the first quest because 'The Prophecy of Gray' dictated it. This has been deemed too unnecessarily dangerous for a queen," Luxa said, glancing at Vikus.

Gregor thought she at least could have put up an argument. Maybe even Luxa wasn't keen on chasing down the Bane. It made him kind of mad, though.

"So, who's going, then?" asked Gregor.

"Well, first you should know that we had no lack of volunteers," Vikus said, as if to reassure Gregor that this was going to be a guaranteed good time. "But the openings were very limited. Besides yourself, Ares, Boots, Temp, and Twitchtip, we will be sending Mareth and Howard and their fliers."

"Howard?" said Gregor. He liked Mareth a lot, but he didn't want Luxa's cousin going along. Howard was part of that Fount crowd, and who knew if he'd ever seen a rat — besides that dead one on the beach?

"Apart from being a most excellent fighter, he is well versed in the ways of water travel," said Solovet. "We are most fortunate his visit coincided with yours."

"Uh-huh," said Gregor. "So Ripred's not coming, either?" Nobody made him feel safer than Ripred . . . when he wasn't wondering if the big rat would kill him.

"He left this morning for the Dead Land," said Vikus. "Oh, I see the boats are loaded! We had best get you on your way!"

Ares landed beside them. "The river is too hazardous. We will fly to the Waterway and then board the boats."

"Glad you're coming, anyway," Gregor muttered, shooting a resentful look at Luxa and, while he was at it, Vikus. He climbed on Ares's back.

Dulcet handed Boots up to him with a slight sound of exertion. "Oh! Boots, you have been growing well!"

"I big girl! I ride bat! I ride bat!" Boots squealed in delight, bouncing in front of Gregor. On the first trip, Gregor had carried her in a backpack, but she was getting too big for that, especially with the life jacket.

"Temp ride, too!" said Boots. The cockroach scurried up behind them, his movements somewhat restricted by his bulky flotation device.

Twitchtip slid into one of the big boats and flattened herself in the middle. Her nose poked over the side, trying to catch the breeze that blew up the river. Gregor felt a twinge of sympathy for the rat. She might be the only one more miserable about this journey than he was.

Teams of bats lifted the two loaded boats by rope loops and started down the river. As Ares took off after them, Gregor wrapped his arms tightly around Boots. He was becoming familiar with the journey now, the fading lights of Regalia, the glimmer as they passed the crystal-walled beach where he had had his first encounter with rats, and finally the wide-open expanse of the Waterway.

They flew a few miles out over the Waterway before the teams of bats lowered the boats into the water and took off. Howard's bat landed in the boat with Twitchtip. Ares settled in the second boat, as did Mareth's bat.

"This is Andromeda. She is my bond," Mareth said, touching his hand to the wing of his gold-and-black-speckled bat. Gregor remembered Mareth had been riding her during the rat fight back on the crystal beach. She'd been so badly injured that she had not come on "The Prophecy of Gray" trip. Gregor still felt kind of responsible for that fight because it had happened when he'd tried to escape.

"Hey, nice to meet you," he said. Did she still blame him for that night?

"I am honored to meet you also, Overlander," she said. Maybe, like Mareth, she had forgiven him.

Mareth also introduced him to Howard's bond, Pandora, a graceful bat with beautiful rusty red fur. All she said to him was "Greetings."

Vikus had flown out after them to bid them good-bye. "Gregor, I forgot to deliver you this," he called. His large gray bat swooped over Gregor's boat, and something fell to the floor. Gregor picked up a scroll and found a copy of "The Prophecy of Bane" written in Nerissa's elegant hand.

"Fly you high!" Vikus headed back toward Regalia, giving them an encouraging wave. Gregor managed a nod back.

Boots was wriggling madly to get out of Gregor's arms. Letting her loose in the boat made him nervous, but he couldn't hold her for days at a time. He set her down on the floor with strict instructions to "Stay in the boat!"

Fortunately the vessel was so deep that she couldn't get out, anyway. When Gregor stood in the middle, the sides rose up to his shoulders. It was about twenty feet long and made of some kind of animal hide stretched over a bone frame. A two-foot-wide strip of floor ran down the center of the boat. About a third of the way from the front of the boat, Mareth hoisted a wooden mast into the air and secured it at the hinged base. It was only the second wooden object Gregor had seen used in the Underland, the first being the door to Sandwich's room. There were a few seats fashioned from leather, and a lot of supplies. Especially food.

"Are we really going to eat all this?" asked Gregor.

"Not by ourselves. But the shiners will require a great deal of food," said Mareth.

"The shiners?" said Gregor.

"Vikus did not tell you?" began Mareth.

Gregor wondered how many times he was going to hear that in the next few days.

"On long voyages, we cannot carry enough fuel to provide light. So we hire shiners to aid us," said Mareth. "They should be here directly — yes, see . . . here they come now."

Gregor looked out into the dark and spotted two points of light. They went out, and then turned on again, closer this time. As the flickering light continued to approach, he could make out the forms of flying insects. By the time the two giant bugs had landed on the bows of the boats, he had identified them.

"Oh, they're fireflies!" he said. Back at his dad's family's farm in Virginia, they flew at the edge of the woods at night. Their little twinkling lights made the whole place look magical. The three-foot-tall versions perched on the boat weren't nearly so enchanting. But he had to admit that when their butts lit up, they put out some light.

"Greetings, Shiners," said Mareth with a bow.

"Greetings, all," one of the fireflies said in a high and impossibly whiny voice. "I am he called Photos Glow-Glow and she is Zap."

"It was my turn to make the introduction," wailed Zap. "Photos Glow-Glow made it last time."

"But we both know that, as a male, I am more visually pleasing to humans," Photos Glow-Glow said, his rear end blinking in a variety of colors. "Zap can only make one color, and it is yellow."

"I hate you!" shrieked Zap.

And Gregor knew this was going to be the longest trip of his life.

11

Gregor had never bitten his nails before, but he started doing it about five minutes after the fireflies arrived. They were unbelievable! They argued about where they would sit, they argued about who should take the first shift, they even argued about whose servant Temp should be since he was obviously just a no-account crawler, until the roach spoke up with uncharacteristic force, "Only the princess, Temp serves, only the princess."

Mareth tried to feed them to distract them, but they just bickered about each other's table manners.

"Must you talk with your mouth full, Zap?" Photos Glow-Glow said. "It kills my appetite."

"This from someone who just sat in his milk!" Zap said, and apparently she had him there, because his rear end went bright red in anger, and he chomped on a mushroom in silence for at least thirty seconds.

"Are they always like this?" Gregor whispered to Mareth.

"In truth, these two are not as bad as some others I have traveled with," whispered back Mareth. "I once saw a pair try to fight to the death over a piece of cake."

"Try to?" said Gregor.

"They are not very capable fighters, and they tire quickly. So they ended up accusing each other of cheating, and giving up. Then they sulked for several days," said Mareth.

"Do we really need them?" asked Gregor.

"Unfortunately, yes," said Mareth.

Even Boots, who had stationed herself on the floor of the boat to roll a ball around with Temp, seemed aggravated by the newcomers.

"Fo-Fo, too loud!" she said, tugging on one of his wings. "Shh, Fo-Fo!"

"Fo-Fo? Fo-Fo? I am he called Photos Glow-Glow and will answer to no other name!" said Photos Glow-Glow.

"She's just a little kid. She can't say Photos Glow-Glow," said Gregor.

"Well, then, I cannot understand her!" said the firefly.

"Allow me to translate," Twitchtip said, not even bothering to move. "She said if you don't stop your incessant babble, that big rat sitting in the boat next to you will rip your head off."

The silence that followed was blissful. Gregor felt positively friendly toward Twitchtip, and decided he wouldn't mind riding in her boat at all.

They were far out into the Waterway now. The torches had been extinguished when the shiners arrived, and the fireflies' glow only illuminated the immediate area. Gregor snapped on his best flashlight for a minute and shone it around. All signs of land had vanished.

There were waves, too, now. And even a decent breeze. Mareth and Howard ran silken sails up the masts and were preoccupied with steering the two vessels. Their bats settled comfortably together and dozed off. Gregor noticed that Ares didn't join them. On the first quest, all the bats had gathered in a clump to sleep together after flights. But maybe Ares wasn't welcome now.

"Hey, Ares, do you know how long it will take us to get to the Labyrinth in this boat?" asked Gregor.

"At least five days," said Ares. "If we flew, we could make it in less time, but it is believed that very few bats could make the journey. No one has ever tried it."

"I bet you could make it," said Gregor. He meant it, too. Henry hadn't chosen Ares just because he was a troublemaker; the bat was also impressively strong and swift.

"I have thought that I might try it someday, to see if I could accomplish it," admitted Ares.

"Like Lindbergh. He's the first guy who flew across the Atlantic Ocean by himself," said Gregor.

"He had wings?" asked Ares.

"Well, mechanical ones. He was a person. He had a plane. That's a machine that flies. Now people fly across the ocean all the time in great big planes, but not when Lindbergh was flying," said Gregor.

"He is famous, in the Overland?" asked Ares.

"Yeah, I mean, he was. He's dead now, but he was real famous. People were mad at him, too. Because of something about a war," Gregor said, unsure about that part. There was a sad thing, too, about a baby. But he couldn't remember that exactly, either.

Gregor picked up the scroll with "The Prophecy of Bane" and opened it.

He let the scroll snap shut. He looked at Boots, who was quietly singing "Row Row Row Your Boat" while she drummed on Temp's shell. She was so perfect, somehow, in that way little kids are perfect. So innocent. How did anyone think they were going to solve anything by killing her? And yet at this moment, Gregor knew squads of rats were scouring the Underland to do just that.

"Can rats swim?" Gregor asked, peering out into the water.

"Yes, but not as far out as we are. The rats cannot reach her here," Ares said, following his thoughts.

But eventually they would have to land. And there would be the Bane.

"Have you ever killed a rat?" asked Gregor.

"Not alone. Together with Henry, yes. I flew while he held the sword," said Ares.

Then Gregor remembered he had seen the rat Fangor die on Henry's sword, back on that crystal beach. But it was sort of a blur.

"How do you do it? I mean, where exactly is it best

to . . . where do you stab it?" The words felt strange in his mouth.

"The neck is vulnerable. The heart, but one must get past the ribs. Through the eyes to the brain. Under the foreleg is a vein that bleeds greatly. If you strike at the belly, you may not kill instantly, but the rat will likely die within days from infection," said Ares.

"I see," said Gregor. But he didn't. That is, he couldn't really see himself doing it. Killing the giant white rat. The whole thing was surreal.

"Is it okay if I'm riding you? Or do I have to be on the ground?" asked Gregor.

"I will be there, if it is at all possible," said Ares.

"Thanks," said Gregor. "Sorry I got you into this mess."

"You also freed me from one," said Ares. And they left it at that.

Mareth called a dinner break and passed around food. The fireflies ate with gusto, even though they had just been fed.

After everyone had eaten, Mareth lowered the sails in his boat and hooked the front of his craft to the back of Howard's with a towrope. "Howard and I will take turns sailing the lead boat while the rest sleep.

But we need someone on guard and one shiner on duty at all times."

"Zap will take the first shift," said Photos Glow-Glow. "My light requires more energy."

"It is a lie!" howled Zap. "I can only make one color, but the effort is the same. He only says this so that he will be given more food and less work!"

"Photos Glow-Glow will take the first shift," said Twitchtip. "Or I'll shred his wings into ribbons." So that settled that. "Who wants to watch with him?"

"We are many and can switch guards every two hours or so," said Mareth.

Gregor was wiped out, but he hated the idea of being woken up after an hour or two of sleep and then having to be on guard, so he volunteered to go first.

In the lead boat, Howard took his place by the rudder to steer. His bat folded its wings to sleep. Twitchtip, who had barely moved since they left Regalia, closed her eyes. Zap's soft yellow light faded out, and she began to snore.

Gregor took off Boots's life jacket, wrapped her snugly in a blanket, and settled her down next to Temp in the stern of their boat. Ares perched next to them. Mareth stretched out on the floor, with Andromeda nearby. Photos Glow-Glow turned his bulb to a steady orange light and lit on the bow, a few feet in front of Mareth, illuminating the space between the boats.

Gregor sat on a pile of supplies and laid his forearm across the side of the boat. It was quiet except for the lapping of the waves, soft breathing, and firefly snores. The rocking of the boat had a hypnotic effect. His eyelids felt leaden.

He had barely slept in days . . . the rats were after Boots . . . maybe he could just rest his head on his shoulder . . . he had to kill Ripred . . . no, the Bane . . . he had to kill the Bane . . . how many nights had he been down here? . . . he had to kill somebody. . . .

Boots's cold little hand was wrapping around his wrist. "What, Boots?" he murmured. She was squeezing him now. Squeezing him hard. "What? You need a blanket?"

He tried to pull his arm away. Her fingers dug in deeper, creeping up his arm, causing real pain. Gregor's eyes flew open. Boots was sleeping peacefully next to Temp, yards away from him. He twisted his head to the side.

Curled around his forearm was a slimy red tentacle.

CHAPTER

12

"Aah!" Gregor had just enough time to let out a yell before the tentacle gave a terrific yank. He flew over the side of the boat and would have gone straight into the water if one of his boots hadn't caught on the edge. "Ares!" A second yank pulled him headfirst, under the water up to his waist. He managed to get a good breath of air before he submerged. His legs were sliding under, too, now. He could feel the cold water climbing over his thighs, his knees, his ankles — oh! Someone had him by the feet and was pulling back!

A tug-of-war ensued, with Gregor as the rope. For a dreadful minute it was touch-and-go, with the creature dragging him deeper and Ares dragging him back out. Gregor beat at the tentacle with his free hand, but it didn't seem to have much effect. Finally he got his mouth up to his arm and sank his teeth into the tentacle as deeply as he could. He didn't know if he did any real damage, but he surprised the animal enough for it to loosen its grip a bit. Just then Ares gave a big heave-ho and Gregor flew out of the water, coughing and gasping for air. He dangled upside down a moment, his boots locked in Ares's claws, before the bat dropped him on the floor of the boat. Gregor retched, and a gush of water rushed out of his mouth. He vaguely noticed it was salty, like the ocean.

"Overlander!" he heard Mareth cry. "Can you fight?"

Fight? Gregor struggled onto his hands and knees and got his first good look at their situation.

Tentacles were shooting up over the sides of the boat right and left, their suckers latching on to anything they came in contact with. The crew was fighting back with whatever they had — swords, teeth, claws, pincers — trying to sever the appendages from the ghastly creatures looming in the dark water beneath them.

"Catch!" he heard Mareth yell, and he saw a sword flying at him. He grabbed it out of the air by the handle just in time to slice through a tentacle that had encircled his ankle.

Photos Glow-Glow and Zap were blazing. But even without their help, Gregor could have seen by the light of the water, which shone an unearthly phosphorescent green. "Squid! It's some kind of squid!" he shouted.

The three bats were in flight, diving down and ripping with their claws. Mareth and Howard were slashing away with swords. Twitchtip was a whirlwind of gnashing teeth.

"Overlander, your sister!" he heard Ares warn.

Gregor turned to see Temp, standing over the still-sleeping Boots. The roach's mandibles were snapping away at the intruders. He was disabling many tentacles, but they kept coming. Three grabbed on to the cockroach's life jacket and pulled him into the water, leaving Boots completely unprotected. As Ares dove in to battle for Temp, a particularly large tentacle whipped over the stern.

When Gregor saw the suckers latch on to Boots's blanket, it happened again: the strange phenomenon that had occurred with the blood balls. The greater world receded, and it was as if nothing but he and the tentacles existed. Around him, somewhere, there were voices, and thuds, and glowing green water being beaten into frothy foam. But all he was really aware of was the attackers. His sword began to move — not in a premeditative way, but with some instinctive precision and force utterly beyond his control. He hacked away at tentacle after tentacle after tentacle and —

"Overlander!" He heard Mareth's voice reach out for him. "Overlander, enough!" He didn't stop.

"Ge-go, no hitting! No hitting!" he heard. Boots was crying.

The world zoomed back into perspective. Gregor was standing in the middle of the boat. Severed tentacles flopped on the floor around him. His breath was coming in short, rasping gasps.

Mareth grabbed his shoulders and gave him a sharp shake. "They are going. It is over."

Gregor's arm, the one the squid had caught, not the one holding the sword, throbbed. Four angry red circles, sucker marks, swelled on his forearm. He was drenched with sweat and seawater and squid slime.

"Ge-go, no hitting! Go home! Boots go home!" came from behind him.

He turned out of Mareth's grasp and saw her sitting, still half-tangled in her blanket, sobbing, but unharmed. Muck from the squid had splattered her as well. Temp sat next to her. He was missing two legs.

Gregor tossed away the sword, reached out for Boots, and held her tightly. "Hey, you're okay. You're okay, baby. Don't cry."

"Ge-go, Boots, go home. See Mama," she sobbed. "Ma-ma! Ma-ma!"

That was her ultimate cry of distress. When she was upset and none of the rest of them could fix it. "Mamaa!"

Gregor sunk down on a seat and rocked her back and forth, patting her back, and trying to soothe her with words. How much had she seen? And what had she seen him do?

While he held her on his lap, Howard appeared with a pail of water and cleaned her off. Somehow he distracted her with some silly rhyme about washing her toes.

"TWO TINY ROWS,

OF FIVE TINY TOES,

GIVE BOOTS TEN GOOD REASONS TO WIGGLE HER NOSE."

At this point, Howard would press her foot against his nose, sniff her toes, and go, "Whew!" as if the smell about knocked him out.

"WIGGLE YOUR NOSE,

AT EIGHT, NINE, TEN TOES,

THEN GIVE THEM A BATH SO EACH TINY TOE GLOWS."

Boots began to laugh between sobs, especially whenever Howard said "Whew!" and soon she was completely caught up in trying to say the rhyme with him. Gregor had spent a lot of time amusing his little sisters. He recognized a good toddler bit when he saw it.

"You make that up?" he asked Howard.

"Yes. For Chim. It was always hard to get her to take baths," said Howard, avoiding his gaze. It crossed Gregor's mind that he had not been particularly nice to Howard. He had lumped him in with Stellovet and the other cousins, but Howard hadn't liked what his sister had said to Luxa about Henry. And he had not bragged about their dad being in charge at the Fount.

They got Boots dressed in fresh clothes and gave her a cookie. She trotted off to teach the rhyme to Temp, who lacked not only toes, but legs.

"Temp, do you need some bandages, or medicine?" asked Gregor.

"No. More legs, I will grow, more legs," said Temp. He didn't seem too upset about the loss.

Photos Glow-Glow and Zap were uninjured and very pleased with the bounty of squid parts that littered the boat. Apparently, squid was a real delicacy for fireflies, and the two had no time to squabble as they embarked in a heated race to see who could wolf down the most.

Andromeda and Twitchtip had a couple of sucker marks, but Gregor's were the worst, as the squid had held on to him the longest and he had no fur to protect his skin. As they all cleaned the slime off their bodies, he saw the swollen red circles were beginning to ooze pus. His whole body felt hot and shaky.

"I think maybe it poisoned me or something," Gregor said, and suddenly his knees gave way and he was lying in the boat. Everything was swimming around. Someone pressed something against his lips and ordered him to swallow. He managed to obey just before he blacked out.

A fevered dream followed. He was submerged in bubbly fluorescent green water, wrestling with writhing tentacles, while hideous fish dug their fangs into his arm again and again. His whole family watched over the side of the boat, reaching for him, trying to pull him to safety. He screamed to Boots to get back, but she kept singing the rhyme about her toes. Temp appeared in the water beside him, bobbing around in his life jacket. He pulled off his legs, offering them to Gregor. At some point, thankfully, he sank into nothingness.

When he came to, he could tell that a lot of time had passed. His arm was bandaged and pulsating with pain. It hurt to open his eyes.

And when he did, he had a moment of confusion.

For there, sitting in the bow of the boat and smiling down at him, was Luxa.

CHAPTER
13

"I let you go off for one day, and look at the trouble you get into," Luxa said.

"I bet I know somebody else who's in trouble," Gregor croaked with a smile.

"Much trouble," he heard Mareth say behind him. Gregor didn't have to turn his head to see the soldier's expression. He was angry.

"I cannot go back," Luxa said with satisfaction. "It is too far now, and Aurora and I would most surely perish in the deep."

"Yes, you timed that nicely," said Mareth.

"I know," said Luxa.

"I know you know. Everyone will know you knew if you ever arrive home in one piece to tell the tale," said Mareth. Gregor had never thought much about

Mareth's relationship with Luxa. She was his queen, or would be when she turned sixteen, but there was another side to it he recognized after the day of training. Mareth was her coach, and he wasn't afraid to chew her out.

"Oh, Mareth, how long are you to stay angry with me?" said Luxa. "It has been at least a day already. No one will blame you for my disobedience."

"That is much beside the point, Luxa!" barked Mareth. "This venture is extremely dangerous, and what if you die? You leave Regalia with Nerissa as a leader, and she is of age. Can you imagine what will happen then? To Regalia? To Nerissa?"

"She will have to abdicate," Howard said from somewhere in the other boat.

"She will do no such thing. She will rule if I die and not Vikus, and never you and your wretched sister!" said Luxa.

There was a shocked silence. Then Howard spoke. "Is this what you think? That I want to be king? I believe you have me confused with another cousin."

Ouch. It was another allusion to Henry. But this time, Gregor thought Luxa might have had it coming.

"And do not judge me by Stellovet. She is wretched.

I admit it. But I can no more control her than you could control Henry!" Howard spat out.

"If you think I will believe you innocent, I will not. I have seen you torment Nerissa," said Luxa.

"When? When did I do this? I have barely spent five minutes with her altogether!" said Howard.

"At the festival. When you set that lizard at her!" said Luxa.

"Set it? I did not set it! That was a rare color changer, and I thought it would amuse her to see it!" said Howard.

"But Henry said he saw you — !" began Luxa.

"Henry said? *Henry* said? I cannot believe that even now you do not question things that Henry said, Luxa! Is he the one who told you I was after your crown?" Howard's voice rose in frustration. "Henry said!"

"Shh. Too loud. You like Fo-Fo," he heard Boots say.

"It is Photos Glow-Glow!" said an offended voice in the next boat.

"Oh, be quiet, Fo-Fo," said Twitchtip, and Gregor had to pretend to cough to conceal he was laughing.

Boots's feet pattered up by Gregor's head. She leaned over, looking upside down at him. "Hi, you!"

"Hi, you," said Gregor. "What's going on, Boots?"

"I do toes. Whew! I do bekfast. Two times," Boots said, holding up four fingers. She squatted down and pressed her nose into his forehead so their eyes were blinking at each other upside down. "I see you," she said.

"I see you, too," said Gregor.

"Bye," Boots said, and trotted off to the other end of the boat.

Gregor struggled to a sitting position. His whole body ached like he had the flu. He leaned against the side of the boat and looked at his bandaged arm. "So, what's it look like under the bandage?"

"It is not for the faint of heart," said Mareth. "You may thank Howard for saving your arm."

"Saving it? You were going to cut it off?" Gregor asked, instinctively pulling it closer.

"We would have had no choice if the venom spread further, but Howard was able to suck it from the wounds," said Mareth.

"Ugh. Thanks, Howard," Gregor said, gingerly flexing his fingers. Luxa scowled at him. "What? He sucked venom from my arm! I can't say thank you?"

"I am trained in water aid. I have sworn to save anyone in peril related to the water," said Howard.

"If my cousin had been paying attention that night, there would be no need to be so grateful," said Luxa.

Gregor remembered waking, seeing the tentacle. . . . "No, it was my fault. I was supposed to be on guard and I . . . I fell asleep." He felt ashamed to admit it, but it wasn't fair to let Howard take the blame.

Everyone was quiet for a minute, then Mareth spoke up. "We probably would still have been attacked. But it is crucial to stay awake on guard. Not only our own survival, but that of many hangs on this journey."

It was even worse than Gregor thought, then. "Sorry. I was tired, but I thought I could stay awake."

"It is something you learn, how to stand guard. There are tricks to keeping your mind alert. You will find them," said Howard. But Luxa and Mareth said nothing, and Gregor knew that, for them, what he had done was inexcusable. Howard came from the Fount; it was not so dangerous there. Luxa and Mareth had fought too many rats to let him off the hook.

Mareth called a break for dinner. Gregor was famished. He stuffed way too much in his mouth, choked, and had to take a piece of bread back out. "Excuse me. I guess I haven't eaten since dinner last night."

"That was two nights ago," said Howard. "You have been out for almost two full days."

"Two days!" exclaimed Gregor. He had never been out that long before. Two days, plus the one he had traveled. They must be at least halfway to the Bane, and he felt no more prepared to face it than when he had left Regalia. He should be doing something! He thought about asking Mareth to give him a few more sword lessons, but he was so wiped out from the squid venom, he doubted he could lift the sword.

Besides, hitting things with a sword didn't seem to be his problem. In fact, if anything, he couldn't stop hitting things. It was like something took over his whole being, something beyond his control.

In a weak attempt to better his chances with the Bane, he lay on his back for a while, practicing echo-location. Click! But his mind kept going back to the squid and how he hadn't been able to stop hacking away at it. He couldn't really even remember fighting it, the same way he couldn't really remember hitting all the blood balls. Click! Sometimes that happened to people who were crazy. . . . They had blank spots and couldn't remember how they'd gotten somewhere or what they'd been doing. Click! Oh, and there was that guy in that werewolf movie, same thing happened to him. He'd just wake up all bloody, wondering what had happened to his clothes. Click! Gregor knew there weren't really werewolves. Click! Then again, how did he know that? If you'd asked him six months ago, he'd have said there weren't giant, talking rats!

Click! Click! Click!

He was getting nowhere with this echolocation stuff. Maybe Ripred was right, he had to focus. But who could focus when they were in the middle of an underground sea, full of squid venom, on their way to killing a monstrous white rat? Not him.

Gregor sat up and saw Luxa sitting nearby, sharpening her sword on some kind of stone.

"How do you feel?" she asked.

"Better since I ate," said Gregor.

Luxa tested the edge of her blade by splitting a strand of rope. She frowned in dissatisfaction and continued to work on it.

"That looks pretty sharp to me," said Gregor.

"Not sharp enough for what lies ahead of us," said Luxa. "It is doubtful many of us will survive."

"So why did you come?" asked Gregor.

"I thought you might need my help. You have depended on it before," said Luxa. "And Aurora and I, we have Ares to think of as well."

While all of that might be true, Gregor had a feeling there was more going on inside Luxa. "Is that all?"

"Is that not enough?" Luxa asked, avoiding his gaze.

"Sure, I just thought, well, maybe it had something to do with . . ." Gregor stopped himself.

"With what?" said Luxa.

"With nothing," said Gregor. "Forget it."

"I can hardly forget it now," said Luxa. "Why else would I come?"

"Because of Henry. I mean, if I were you, I might come to show people I wasn't like him. I might come to make Stellovet shut up," said Gregor.

Luxa didn't admit that what he said was right, but she didn't deny it, either.

"So, what's the deal with who gets to be king and queen here?" Gregor asked after a while.

"My father's family has been on the throne for some time. As his only child, I am to rule next. If I have children, the oldest will follow me," said Luxa.

"Even if it's a girl and she has brothers?" Gregor

thought that girls only got to rule if there were no boys in the family.

"Oh, yes. Girls have equal claim to the throne," said Luxa. "If I have no children, the crown will go to Nerissa. But she is the last in our line. So if she dies, or abdicates without children, Regalia will have to choose a new royal family."

"And Stellovet thinks it will be her family," said Gregor.

"She is probably right. Vikus and Solovet will be the most likely choice. Their oldest child, my aunt Susannah, would follow. And then her children, my Fount cousins. Howard is the eldest," said Luxa.

"Sounds like Stellovet's a long way from being queen, anyway," said Gregor.

"Not as long as you might think. Not in the Underland," said Luxa.

The bats, who had been out flying around, came in for bedtime. Mareth put Howard's red bat, Pandora, and Ares on guard. Gregor had a feeling he wasn't going to be assigned that duty for a while.

Twitchtip was restless. "Something's not right," she said. She lifted her nose into the air, and her head made an involuntary jerk to the side.

"Is it more squid?" Gregor asked, looking into the deep.

"No, it's not animal. But something's not right," she repeated.

"In what way?" asked Ares.

"With the water," she said.

"Is it tainted? Frigid? Filled with debris?" asked Howard.

"No," said Twitchtip. "I'd recognize those things. It's something I don't have a word for." But she could not explain further, so there was nothing to do but settle down to an uneasy sleep.

A few hours later, Gregor awoke to the sound of rushing water and Howard's frantic voice screaming the word that Twitchtip didn't have:

"Whirlpool!"

CHAPTER
14

Whirlpool? The only thing Gregor could think of was that game. His cousins had an old, round, aboveground pool. All the kids would try to run around in a circle and make the water swirl around so there was a sort of funnel effect in the middle. He knew there were real whirlpools in the ocean, but he'd never even seen a picture of one.

Gregor jumped to his feet and tried to make sense of the situation. Everyone was up, but they were confused, too. The Underlanders usually faced an emergency with precision, as if they'd drilled for the crisis a million times. Gregor had a feeling that none of them had ever dealt with a whirlpool, either . . . and that they had no emergency response at the ready.

Photos Glow-Glow and Zap were burning at full brightness, but there still wasn't enough light to see far out into the water. Gregor pulled out the biggest flashlight he had, one with a wide sweeping beam, and clicked it on. What he saw took his breath away.

The boats were on the outer edge of a huge vortex. The whirlpool must have been at least a hundred yards wide. The water was rushing at a dizzying speed, grasping at anything in its reach, carrying it around and around until it was sucked down into a black gaping hole in the center.

Howard and Mareth were shouting at each other across the rope that tethered the two boats together.

"I am cutting loose!" Howard yelled as he began to hack away at the rope between them.

"No!" Mareth cried. "The fliers will carry us out!"

"They can only take one boat! Do it, Mareth! Pandora can come back for me!" Howard shouted, and the rope severed under his sword. It was just in the nick of time. The lead boat containing Howard, Pandora, Twitchtip, and Zap was snagged by the outer ring of the whirlpool and carried off into the maelstrom.

It was only a matter of seconds before the second boat would meet the same fate. Gregor lunged for the stern for Boots, who was half-asleep, so he could get her back in her life jacket. He'd taken it off so she could sleep comfortably. Obviously that had been a bad decision. He fumbled with the jacket's tangled straps.

The boat suddenly yanked to the side. "It's got us!" Gregor cried out. But then there was an upward jerk. Gregor sprawled forward, barely avoiding crushing Boots, and found they were rising out of the water. The bats! The bats were lifting them using the rope loops on the sides of the boats. Aurora and Andromeda were in the front, Ares and Pandora in the back.

"Go, Pandora. Ares can take it! Go!" Gregor heard Mareth order.

Ares spread his feet, holding his own loop in one claw and grasping Pandora's in his other. The boat dipped down a bit, but the big black bat soon had it under control. "Man, he's strong!" thought Gregor.

Pandora hovered for one moment, to make sure Ares had things covered, then dove. Gregor leaned over the side of the boat to see what was going on.

They were fifty feet above the water now, safe from the clutches of the raging whirlpool, but below them it was another matter. The lead boat, with Howard and Twitchtip clinging to the mast, was spinning helplessly around in the whirlpool, smashing into debris, buckling under the pressure of the current. Except for the light from Gregor's flashlight, the boat was in complete darkness.

"This is certainly an inconvenience," said a whiny voice by his ear. Gregor turned to see Zap sitting on a coil of rope. "It was my time to sleep, too. I hope Photos Glow-Glow does not think this means I will cover his next shift."

"Zap! What are you doing? Get down there so they can see!" said Gregor.

"Oh, no. We never agree to go into dangerous situations. We are not fed enough for that," said Photos Glow-Glow. And then he actually yawned.

Gregor spun back around to the whirlpool in time to see Howard launch himself out over the water, arms straight out to his sides. Pandora caught him by the arms and carried him straight up to safety. She set Howard in a soggy pile on the floor and took her rope handle back from Ares.

Down in the water, Twitchtip still clung desperately to the mast. The boat was quickly approaching the inner rings of the whirlpool and the black hole in the center.

"Wait a minute!" Gregor cried. "Aren't you going back in for Twitchtip?"

There was no answer. He looked to Mareth, to Luxa, to Howard dripping and panting on the floor. Something in their faces made a chill go through him. "She's going to drown, you know! We've got to get in there!"

"It is not possible, Overlander," said Mareth. "We cannot reach her by boat. A single flier could not get hold of her. It is not possible."

"Luxa?" said Gregor. She was a queen; she could probably make them if she wanted to.

"I think Mareth is right. We will risk more loss in the effort, and the likelihood of success is almost nonexistent," said Luxa.

"But we need her! We need her to navigate in the Labyrinth!" said Gregor. Why were they just standing there?

"The bats will be sufficient," said Mareth. "And they can be trusted."

So, that was it. Now he understood. "It's because she's a rat," he said. "You're just going to sit here and watch her drown because she's a rat, right? If it were Howard or Andromeda or even Temp, you'd be down there, all right, but not for a rat! You'd probably have killed her already if you could have!"

Below him, Twitchtip's boat snapped in two. She clung to the wreckage for a few seconds, and then it was swept out of her grasp. She clawed her way through the water, fighting to keep from going under, but she wouldn't last long.

The life jacket was on the floor next to Boots. He shoved his arms through the straps and buckled it with shaking hands. The small flashlight, the one Mrs. Cormaci had given him, was in his pocket. He flicked it on. Maybe he could hold it between his teeth.

Hands grabbed him as he climbed up the side of the boat. "Do not be a madman, Overlander," said Howard. "You cannot help her!"

"You make me the sickest of all!" said Gregor. "You were just down there a minute ago. You got rescued! And what about what you swore? About saving anyone in water trouble! In peril! What you said! What about that?"

Howard's face flushed. Gregor had touched a nerve.

"Gregor!" Luxa had his hand. "I forbid you to go, Gregor! You will not survive."

"Not with you guys as backup!" said Gregor. He was so furious, he could have thrown her over the side of the boat. See how she liked it down there. "Ripred brought her for me. He brought her to help me, so I could help you guys and your whole stupid kingdom!" he said. "That's why we're doing this, right?"

He stood on one of the seats and shone his light down in the water. Man! Was he really going to jump down into that? They were right, it was insane. Even if he'd been the best Olympic swimmer in the world, he'd never swim his way out of that, especially pulling some big old rat. But he knew something else, too. He knew that the Underlanders needed to keep him alive at all costs. If he went in, they'd come after him. And if he could get to Twitchtip, they'd have to save them both.

Howard started lashing something around his body.

"Untie me!" Gregor said, taking a swing at him.

"It is a lifeline!" Howard said, ducking the blow. "We will hold on to you from this end!"

"You will?" said Gregor.

"Do not fight the current. It will have no effect. Ride it as best you can!" said Howard.

Gregor balanced on the edge of the boat for one second, stuck his flashlight between his teeth, braced himself, tried to forget about how much he hated high dives, and jumped.

The shock of the cold water occupied him for about a millisecond before all his attention was on the current. He was nothing — a twig, a gum wrapper, an ant being carried along by the immense force of the whirlpool. He felt himself yanked back up by the rope. They had him from above.

He was being lifted, swung out over the dark, sucking hole at the center of the whirlpool. For a moment, he had the crazy idea that they were going to drop him into it, and then he understood. Twitchtip was on the inner rings of the vortex. Maybe one, maybe two times more around, and then she was gone.

As they swung him in to meet her, Gregor tried to think of how he could get hold of the rat. There was no time to work out a strategy. As he came in, he did the one thing that came naturally: He opened his arms. They smacked into each other, chest to chest. His arms encircled her neck, his legs wrapped around her body. Twitchtip dug her claws into the front of the life jacket. They spun around the whirlpool again. The current locked on them, pulling them down, not wanting to let them go.

"They can't do it!" thought Gregor. "We're going under!" He squeezed his eyes shut tightly, waiting to be engulfed. Instead, there was a rib-crushing tug and suddenly they were swinging free. Twitchtip's full weight hit him. If the rat hadn't gotten one claw embedded in the rope, he would have lost her.

"Don't — let — go!" she choked out.

Gregor couldn't free his teeth from the flashlight, he had bitten down so hard. He managed to open his mouth enough to say, "No."

They were carried over the water for a while, until they were out of the whirlpool's reach. Then they were in the waves, half-treading water, half-using the life jacket to stay afloat, as the Underlanders reeled them in. Hands pulled them into the boat. When he felt the floor beneath him, he released the rat.

They lay side by side, gasping, coughing up water. This was extra tricky for Gregor, since his teeth were still stuck in his flashlight. His ribs hurt from the final tug that had freed them. He hoped they were just bruised, not broken. If they ached, the pain was minimal compared to his arm. The bandage had been torn away by the current, and Gregor could see it in all its glory. The whole forearm was badly swollen. The sucker wounds, which had turned a revolting shade of purple, oozed fluorescent green pus. They burned as if they were on fire.

Howard was at his side. He helped Gregor free his teeth from the flashlight and laid it on the floor. Gregor had a funny memory. When Mrs. Cormaci had given him the flashlight, she had made a point of telling him it was waterproof. It even had a little sticker on the bottom that said so. He'd thought at the time that was silly, why would he need a waterproof flashlight? Now he knew.

Gregor gritted his teeth as Howard flushed out the wounds on his arm, poured a cooling solution over the skin, and bandaged it in fresh fabric.

"I know this comes a bit late," said Howard. "But try to keep it dry." There was something in his eyes that reminded Gregor of Howard's grandfather, Vikus. An odd twinkle, even while the rest of his face remained serious.

Gregor couldn't help laughing. "Yeah. I'll do that."

Howard toweled off Twitchtip and wrapped her in blankets. She was too exhausted to object when he poured a bottle of medicine down her throat. She went to sleep almost immediately.

"Is she all right?" Gregor asked him.

"Yes. We must keep her warm. The cold water has been a shock. But she is a fighter," Howard said with respect.

Boots came up and stuck a cookie in Gregor's mouth. "You wet."

"Yeah," he said, spraying crumbs as he talked.

"Boots go swim? We go swim?" she said hopefully. Gregor was glad she hadn't been able to see over the side of the boat.

"Nah. It's too cold," said Gregor. "I tried it, and it's too cold, Boots."

Boots took a bite of a second cookie and poked the rest in Gregor's mouth. "Yesterday? We go yesterday?" She got time all mixed up. Yesterday, today, tomorrow, later, before — all pretty much meant anytime that wasn't right now.

"Maybe when we get home. And it gets warm again. I'll take you to the pool, okay?" said Gregor.

"Ye-es!" said Boots. She patted his chest. "You wet."

Gregor got on some dry clothes and wrapped himself up in a blanket. He had to take his boots off for a while. They were waterproof, but not in a whirlpool.

The boat was packed now, with all thirteen of them in it. Somehow everyone had found a place, but it was tight.

Luxa sat next to Gregor and handed him something. "Here. I made you a sandwich."

He looked down at the clunky version of a roast beef sandwich. He had taught her to make her first sandwich on their last trip. "Thanks." He didn't eat it.

"Do not be angry with us, Gregor. Mareth and I have lost more than you know to the rats. It is hard for us to risk anything to save one. Even if it is of use," said Luxa.

"*She*. Twitchtip is a *she*. And she's had a bad time, too. The rats chased her out because she's a scent seer and she's been living all alone in the Dead Land," said Gregor.

"Has she?" asked Luxa. "I did not know this about her."

"Well, no, because no one talks to her!" Gregor said, and then had a pang of guilt. He hadn't been talking to her, either. He hadn't wanted to ride in her boat. At least he'd gone in to save her. "But she's incredible. You should see her in action. I mean, maybe she didn't know what a whirlpool was. But she could tell all the way from the arena to the palace what color shirt Boots was wearing. And once we're in that Labyrinth thing, I think she's the only way we'll find the Bane!" His words were tumbling out now; he couldn't stop them, but he couldn't organize them quite right, either. "And . . . and . . . Ripred brought her. Vikus told me once he had wisdom . . . wisdom unique . . . well, more wisdom than, like . . . practically anyone, okay? So, if he brought her, we must need her. And, anyway, besides that . . . besides that . . . it's no good, Luxa!" He paused to get it right. "It's no good to sit up in the boat and watch her drown."

Gregor took a bite of the sandwich — more to stop talking than anything. It was all so confusing, the whole thing with the rats and the humans. They had killed Luxa's parents, and he didn't know how many others she loved. Another thought struck him. "Helping a rat doesn't make you like Henry, you know."

"You see it that way. Others might not," she said.

They sat in silence while he ate his sandwich. He couldn't argue with her there.

Gregor found a spot on the floor at the front of the boat and made a bed out of blankets. Ares landed on a nearby seat.

"Hey, Ares," he said. "What's up?"

"I am unsettled. About your rescuing the rat," said Ares.

"Oh, great," thought Gregor. "Here we go again." But he had it all wrong.

"I could not let go of the boat. I would have dived for you, but I could not let go of the boat without everyone falling," Ares said, his wings fluttering in distress.

"Well, I know that," said Gregor. "Of course, you couldn't. I didn't expect you to."

"I did not want you to think, as your bond, that I would not come after you," said Ares. "The way I did not go after Henry."

"I didn't. I mean, I don't. You've already come after me way more than I've come after you," said Gregor. "You did the only thing you could do."

Gregor sat on his makeshift bed. Boots climbed onto his lap and gave a big yawn. "I seepy."

"Yeah, me, too. Let's get some shut-eye, okay?" He lay down with Boots in the crook of his good arm and pulled a blanket over them.

"We shut eyes," Boots said, and snuggled off to sleep.

Gregor had neglected to put the life jacket back on her again. He really didn't think she could sleep in it, anyway. But what if they ran into another squid or whirlpool or something?

"Hey, Ares," he said. "If something bad happens again? I need you to promise me something."

"What is this promise?" said the bat.

"Save Boots. I mean, save her before me. I know we're bonds and all, but get her first," said Gregor.

Ares thought about it for a minute. "I will save both of you."

"But if you have to choose one of us, choose Boots, okay?" said Gregor. There was no answer. "Please, Ares."

The bat sighed. "I will save her over you, if I must choose, if this is what you wish."

"This is what I wish," Gregor said, letting go and relaxing into sleep. He felt better knowing Ares was there, watching out for Boots, too. Maybe between him and Ares and, of course, Temp, they could keep her safe.

Hours later, when Gregor awoke, he felt a warm body pressed up against his leg. He wriggled his arm, which had gone numb, out from under Boots's head and sat up. In the light of Photos Glow-Glow's bulb, he could see Twitchtip lying against him. He gave a little start of surprise, and she opened her eyes.

Twitchtip looked embarrassed and scooted away about six inches, which was as much as the close confines of the boat would allow. It was this reaction that gave Gregor the idea that she hadn't just rolled over against him in her sleep. She had, at some point, intentionally curled up against his leg. And it led him to another thought. How hungry for contact must Twitchtip be to lean up against him? A human? A human whose scent made her ill? She must be starved. All those years of living alone in the Dead Land had left her desperate to touch any warm being. Even him.

He immediately covered for her. "Hey, sorry. I must've rolled into you when I was sleeping."

"It's hard not to," said Twitchtip. "There's so little room in the boat."

"Yeah," said Gregor. He looked around. Mareth was in the back, steering. Andromeda stood guard next to him. Photos Glow-Glow was perched on the bow, occasionally shifting the color of his rear end. Everyone else was fast asleep.

Gregor considered going back to sleep, but he felt too alert. Besides, this might be a good time to talk to the rat. He tried to think of a way to start the conversation, but Twitchtip began it herself.

"I know you made them save me," said Twitchtip.

"Well, I kind of spearheaded the whole thing," said Gregor, not wanting her to know how readily the others would have let her die.

But she knew, anyway. "Ripred was right about you. He said I couldn't judge you like I would other humans."

"That's interesting. Because I think Vikus said something similar to me about Ripred," said Gregor.

The subject made him uncomfortable. "So how long have you been living on your own?"

"Three or four years," said Twitchtip.

"Why'd they drive you out? The other rats. I mean, they're so into smell, seems like you'd be famous," said Gregor.

"I was, in a way, for some time. Then they realized I could smell their secrets, and no one wanted me around," said Twitchtip. "I can smell yours, too."

"My secrets? Like what?" asked Gregor. He tried to think about what his secrets might be. His father's disappearance used to be a kind of secret, or at least it was something he never discussed much. But that was over. Of course now, the Underland was a secret. But only in the Overland. So what was she talking about?

Twitchtip spoke so softly that Gregor could barely hear her. "I know what happens when you fight."

Gregor was taken aback. But she was right, that was a secret. He hadn't told anybody about how he couldn't really remember what happened once he started swinging a sword. But he didn't let on. "What happens when I fight?" he asked coolly.

"You can't stop. You put out a scent. I have only smelled it once or twice before. We rats have a name for someone like you. You're a rager," said Twitchtip.

"A rager? What's a rager?" asked Gregor. It sounded like somebody who lost their temper a lot.

"It's a special kind of fighter. They're born with great ability. While others may train for years to master combat, a rager is a natural-born killer," said Twitchtip.

It was absolutely the worst thing he could imagine anybody saying about him. "I'm not a natural-born killer!" he gasped. He thought about Sandwich's prophecics, how they called him a warrior, how he was supposed to kill the Bane. "Is that what everybody thinks? I'm some kind of killing machine?"

"No one even knows about it yet, or it would've been the first thing I heard about you. Being a rager — it's not a moral judgment. You can't help being one any more than I can help being a scent seer. It doesn't mean you want to kill, it means you can. Better than anyone. But once you begin to fight, it's very hard for you to rein yourself in," said Twitchtip.

Gregor's heart was pounding. What if she was right? No, she couldn't be right. He didn't even like fighting! He didn't even like people arguing! But what about how he'd acted with the blood balls and the tentacles? He couldn't control what he did. He couldn't even remember it. . . . "I think you've got me mixed up with somebody else" was all he said.

"No, I don't. Ignore me if you want to, but eventually you'll know I'm right. If you get a chance, though, I'd talk to Ripred about it," said Twitchtip.

"Ripred? Why Ripred?" Gregor said, thinking the main person he might need to see was a shrink.

"Because he's a rager, too," said Twitchtip. "But, unlike you, he's learned to control his actions."

Ripred. Well, no question, if anyone was a killing machine, it was that rat. Gregor thought of Ripred whipping his tail at him to check his reflexes and saying, "Well, you can't teach that." Did he already suspect Gregor was a rager? Did Solovet?

"I'm going back to sleep now," Gregor said, and lay down. He pulled Boots close for comfort and stared into the dark. He found himself biting his lip so he wouldn't cry. Yeah. If he got back from this alive, he'd better talk to Ripred.

Hours passed, and slowly, one by one, everyone awoke, and what approximated a "day" in the

Underland began. Gregor had utterly lost track of how long he'd been down here. He thought about asking Luxa, but did he really want to know? Every day down here was a day his family had been suffering at home. His head started to fill with images of that suffering — his dad's illness worsening, his mother's sleepless nights, his sweet grandma's confusion, and Lizzie's fear. What was happening? Did his mom still work every day? Was Lizzie trying to take care of his dad and his grandma and go to school and pretend to Mrs. Cormaci that he and Boots had the flu? Was it almost Christmas? Everything bad was worse at the holidays, he knew that from the years of his dad's absence. All around you were people in an extra-happy mood, and it just made your own hurt bigger. Now that his dad was back, Gregor had thought his family might have one of those merry Christmases again, even if there wasn't a ton of money for presents. And here he was, miles below his home, going to kill a giant white rat and trying to keep his baby sister alive while his family watched the hands crawl around the clock and waited. Ho ho ho.

Besides that, everyone on board was driving one another crazy. It had been an effort for all the different species — human, bat, rat, roach, and firefly — to be cohabiting in two boats. In one boat, it was getting nasty.

Arguments were breaking out right and left, especially over food. A lot of the supplies had been stored in the second boat, so they were lost in the whirlpool. Mareth took stock of the remaining food and put everyone on strict rations. But Photos Glow-Glow and Zap insisted they receive their same gluttonous amounts. When they were told that wasn't going to happen, they whined incessantly until Twitchtip remarked that she could always eat fireflies. Then they simply sulked and only put out light when they felt like it.

"Why do the girl and her flier get our food?" Gregor heard Zap mutter to Photos Glow-Glow. "They are no more than stowaways!"

And of course, Gregor couldn't deny Boots food. When lunch was passed around, she gobbled up her bread and cheese in record time and then pointed at Gregor's. "I hungry!" There was nothing he could do but give her half his food. But after eating that and half of Temp's ration, she was still not full.

"Oh, here, give her this," Twitchtip said, and scooted a chunk of cheese over to Boots, who gnawed on it happily. Everyone gawked at Twitchtip, who snarled. "It reeks of humans, I can barely choke it down, anyway!" And everyone looked away. But Gregor was pretty sure he had witnessed a first — a rat giving a human her food.

Howard was the least concerned about the food issue. "We are surrounded by food, we need only reach in and get it," he said. He lowered nets into the water and sent the bats out to dive for fish. He was right. It didn't take long to assemble a good-sized pile of seafood. Unfortunately, there was no way to cook it. This wasn't a problem for anyone but the humans; most of the others preferred their catch that way. But, raw fish! Gregor stared at the cold, white flesh with distaste. He knew they couldn't waste fuel to cook it. It crossed his mind that he might try warming it up on Photos Glow-Glow's butt, but he didn't like the bug enough to ask.

"You should try it. It is not as bad as you think," Howard said, popping a big piece into his mouth and chewing it up. "Sometimes we serve it this way at the Fount, although it is not done in Regalia."

Gregor nibbled the edge of a chunk and decided it was edible. Then he remembered that a lot of people ate sushi; that was raw fish. He'd walked by Japanese restaurants with beautiful displays of fish and rice and seaweed assembled in bite-sized pieces. It was expensive, too. He'd never had it, but his friend Larry had and he'd said it was okay, if you put a bunch of soy sauce on it. Gregor closed his eyes, pretended he was at a fancy restaurant, and stuck a whole piece in his mouth. He wished he had some soy sauce.

Luxa was trying to get it down, too. Gregor could see she didn't like it much better than he did, but since she wasn't supposed to be here, she couldn't really complain. Besides, she wouldn't want to look like she couldn't handle eating something her cousins could eat.

Boots took a bite and unceremoniously spit it out, then wiped her hand repeatedly over her tongue. "No like! No like!" They were still working on getting her to eat breaded fish sticks with ketchup at home, so that wasn't surprising.

Twitchtip, who had put down about half a dozen fish in a snap, suddenly lifted her head and began to scrunch her nose around. "Land. We're coming to land."

Mareth pulled out a map and scrutinized it. "We should not be, not for several days. I hope the whirlpool has not thrown us off course."

Howard consulted a compass. "No, we are going in the right direction. Can you tell the nature of the land?"

"Perhaps one mile around," Twitchtip said, wriggling her nose.

"Around? Oh, then it is an island?" asked Howard. He pointed to a spot on the map. "I place us here. But there is no island recorded in this area. Although it has been many years since these waters were charted."

"I believe it's recently formed," said Twitchtip. "It has the smell of fresh lava."

"Is there life on it?" asked Mareth.

Twitchtip closed her eyes and concentrated. "Yes, a great deal. No warm-bloods, though. It's all insect. But I don't have a name for their scent."

Gregor started fastening Boots up in her life jacket. The last time Twitchtip didn't have a name for something, they had all almost drowned. An island of unfamiliar insects. That just didn't sound good.

After about another half an hour of sailing, the bats began to raise their heads. Now they were picking up the island on their radar, too.

"How big are the bugs? Can you tell?" asked Gregor. Everything was so oversized here.

"Not large," said Ares. "Tiny, in fact."

That made Gregor feel a little better.

Until Aurora added, "But there are millions of them."

"Can you recognize them, Pandora?" Howard asked.

The bat shook her head. "No, they are most like the mites we encountered on the Island of Shell. But these have a different voice."

"What were the mites like?" asked Gregor.

"Oh, they were harmless. As small as the head of a pin, and while they did bite, it was not lasting," said Howard.

"And they were very tasty," added Pandora. "Not unlike bluebits."

This comment seemed to arouse the interest of all the bats. Whatever bluebits were, Gregor had a feeling that, for bats, they beat out raw fish by a mile.

"Perhaps I should do a flyover. We could get very full, if they are like bluebits," said Pandora.

Mareth was reluctant to let her go, but Howard thought it would be okay. "If they are mites, what harm can they do?"

"Go, I would not, go," Temp said, but no one much ever listened to him.

"Why not, Temp?" asked Gregor. "Do you know what kind of bugs they are?"

Temp didn't. Or he couldn't articulate it if he did. "Bug bad" was all he could say.

"There it is!" Luxa said suddenly, and the place emerged from the darkness. It was visible in the light of a small volcano that slowly bubbled out lava at the center of the island. In a couple of places, the lava spilled over and ran into the water, entering it with a hiss. A junglelike growth of twisted plants covered areas that were not in the lava's path. Gregor guessed they must depend on the light of the lava, since there was no other. Or maybe they only needed its heat. His dad had told him something about that — how they had discovered some things could grow without light if there was heat. Well, whatever they used, these plants were doing fine.

Then there was that hum. The whole place vibrated with life that they couldn't see. Gregor didn't like it. He knew Temp didn't, either. But the other Underlanders seemed curious about the new island.

"It seems a shame to pass it by without any examination," said Howard. "We may gather knowledge that will help future voyagers."

And there was no holding Pandora back. "Yes, it is our duty to at least ascertain if it would make a hospitable place for resting. Some of our stronger fliers could make the crossing, if they knew they might land here."

It was agreed that Pandora could make a quick reconnaissance flight to get a closer look at the place. She flew off swiftly and was soon over the island. It didn't take her long to circle it and report back to the bats in pitches the others couldn't even hear.

"She says it is safe," said Ares. "And the mites are even more delicious than bluebits."

"Well, you may as well fill your bellies," said Mareth. "But only in pairs. I do not like all of you away from the boat at once. You may join her, Ares. Then Aurora and Andromeda may go."

Gregor picked up Boots so she could look, too. It wasn't every day you got to see a volcanic island in an underground ocean. "May as well check it out, if it's safe and all," thought Gregor.

But it wasn't.

Ares was almost to the island when it happened. A black cloud exploded out of the jungle and engulfed Pandora. She had no time to react. One moment she was darting around eating mites, the next moment they were eating her. In less than ten seconds they had stripped the writhing bat down to the bone. Her white skeleton hung for an instant in the air, then crashed into the jungle below.

Then a puzzled little voice next to Gregor's ear asked, "Where bat?"

"Pandora!" Howard cried in horror. "Pan!" He scrambled up over the side of the boat and was about to dive into the water when Mareth yanked him back down.

"Release me, Mareth! We are bonds!" said Howard. He thrashed about wildly in Mareth's grip.

"She is gone, Howard! You cannot help her!" said Mareth.

But Howard was unable to accept this. He twisted out of Mareth's hold and made for the side of the boat again. Mareth grabbed him by the arm, spun him around, and with one punch knocked him unconscious. Luxa caught Howard as he flew backward. She staggered back under his weight, but was able to break his fall as he landed.

In the meantime, Ares, whose first impulse had been to go in to help Pandora, did an abrupt 180-degree turn and began to fly toward open sea for all he was worth. The cloud of mites, which was only a couple of feet from him, rose up into the air and began to chase him. As fast as he flew, the cloud stayed on his tail.

Gregor felt himself hit by the same panic Howard had experienced a few moments before. "Ares!" he cried. "Hurry! They're right behind you!" He felt so helpless. He couldn't jump into the water to save his bat. It would be pointless, and, anyway, Mareth would just knock him out, too. And even if he could get to Ares, how would he stop a cloud of flesh-eating mites? "Think, Gregor!" he said to himself. "What can you do?" The cloud was gaining on Ares now. The black edge was almost touching his tail. They were going to eat him! He was going to be devoured by insects, and his skeleton would fall into the water and — and — wait a minute! That was it!

"Dive, Ares!" Gregor screamed. "Dive into the water!" At first, Gregor wasn't sure the bat had heard him. "Dive!" he shrieked.

And as the mites began to merge over the line of Ares's tail, the bat dove into the water. Gregor wasn't sure exactly what he thought would happen, but it seemed like people sometimes got into water to escape from bugs. Bees and things, anyway. If Ares was in the water, they couldn't get him; that was as far as his plan went. It was somewhat limited in effectiveness since, of course, Ares would soon have to come up for air. But it turned out that Gregor had thought of the right thing, after all, because just then the fish — all the wonderful fish! — surfaced and began to feast on the mites. The cloud halted and began to counterattack the fish. When Ares came up for air, the mites had forgotten him and were busy battling a new enemy and a potential meal.

"Fliers! The ropes!" Mareth ordered, and Aurora and Andromeda grabbed the front loops on the boat and began to drag the vessel through the water. Ares caught up and with him carrying the back end, they soon left the island far behind. Mareth had them fly for several miles before he allowed them to put the boat back in the water and land to rest.

Ares set his end in the water, but did not join them immediately. He dove into the waves again and again, and finally, after about twenty minutes, came in dripping, exhausted and trembling. "The mites," he explained.

"Some of them latched on and were eating me. I believe I have drowned them all now, though."

"Are you okay?" Gregor asked, giving him an awkward pat.

"Yes, I am fine," said Ares. "I have only some small wounds. Not like —" and the bat stopped himself. They all knew who he meant.

Gregor toweled Ares off. Luxa helped him go through the black fur, inch by inch, and apply medicine to wherever the mites had bitten off pieces of his flesh. While they found many wounds, Ares was right. He had left all the bugs in the water.

"It was good, Overlander. Your idea to dive," said Ares.

"Yes, it was very clever to know the fish would come after the mites," said Luxa.

"Well, I hadn't really thought it all the way through to the fish part," admitted Gregor. "Sure glad they were there, though."

When they had finished treating him, Aurora and Andromeda snuggled up against Ares, and the three bats went off to sleep. Gregor was glad Andromeda was no longer shunning his bat. Maybe she'd realized that Aurora would choose Ares over her, and she'd end up alone. Whatever the reason, Gregor thought Ares really needed the company now.

Mareth had his hands full steering the boat, so Gregor and Luxa did their best to tend to Howard as well. He was still out. They made him a bed, covered him up, and took turns holding cold cloths to his swollen jaw.

"Do you think we should try to wake him up?" asked Gregor.

Luxa shook her head. "He has the rest of his life to mourn her."

They were all very quiet that day. The bats slept fitfully, Twitchtip stared out at the water, Mareth steered, Boots and Temp played little games, the fireflies whispered together on the bow and did not complain.

Gregor and Luxa sat side by side, watching Boots and Temp. For a long time, they were silent. Gregor kept reliving Pandora's horrific death in his head and he suspected Luxa was doing the same.

Finally, as if she couldn't stand it anymore, Luxa spoke up. "Tell me about the Overland, Gregor," she said.

"Okay," he said, badly in need of a distraction himself. "What do you want to know?"

"Oh, anything. Tell me . . . what one day is like, from rising to sleep," she said.

"Well, it's really different, depending on who you are," said Gregor.

"Then tell me about one of your days," said Luxa.

So, he did. He told her about the last day he'd been up there, since it was freshest in his mind. He told her about how it was Saturday, so there was no school, and how he'd helped Mrs. Cormaci make scalloped potatoes and bought Lizzie the puzzle book and then had taken Boots sledding. He didn't dwell on the lack of food or his dad's illness, since talking about those things made him feel more anxious and there was enough bad stuff going on around them, anyway. He concentrated on the nicer parts of the day.

Luxa would ask a question here or there, usually if he used an unfamiliar word, but mostly she just listened. When he finished, she sat thoughtfully for a few minutes. Then she said, "I wish I could see the snow."

"You should come on up sometime," Gregor said, and she laughed. "No, really, you should come up for a day. Or a few hours, at least. It's pretty cool, where I live. I mean, it's not a palace or anything. But New York City is something else."

"You do not think Overlanders would find me strange?" asked Luxa.

It was a problem. That translucent skin, those violet eyes . . . "We'll put you in long sleeves and a hat and sunglasses," Gregor said. "You won't look any stranger than about half the people who live there." Suddenly he felt almost enthusiastic about the idea. "And we could go out when it's kind of dark, so the sun won't blind you. I mean, even if we just went down the block and got a slice of pizza, that'd be like nothing you've ever seen!"

They were both happy for a minute. Thinking of being in New York. Thinking of being somewhere else.

Then Luxa sighed and did that thing where she pushed at her crown. "Of course, the council would never permit me to go."

"Oh, yeah, and that's the kind of thing that would stop you," said Gregor.

She gave him a grin and was about to answer when Howard let out a moan.

"Pandora?" he said. Howard sat up so quickly, he had to grab hold of Temp to steady himself. His eyes darted around and landed on the three bats huddled together. He looked upward as if maybe he had dreamt the whole thing and Pandora was flying just overhead.

But of course, she wasn't. "Pandora?" he said. His hand touched his bruised jaw, and he turned to Mareth.

"You could not save her, Howard. None of us could," Mareth said gently.

Gregor could almost see it, the whole weight of Pandora's death coming down on Howard, crushing him. The Underlander dropped his face into his hands and began to sob. It was heartbreaking to watch.

Boots went over and patted him on the back of the neck. "Okay. You okay. You okay, baby," she said soothingly. This was what they said to her when she was upset. Her sweetness only seemed to make Howard cry harder. Boots looked over at her brother. "Ge-go, he cry."

Gregor knew she wanted him to help. To make it better. But he didn't have a clue what to do. Then something unexpected happened.

Luxa stood up, her face paler than usual. She went to her cousin, sat beside him, and put her arms around him. Pressing her forehead into his shoulder, she said, "She will fly with you always. You know this. She will fly with you always."

Howard buried his face in her lap. She leaned her cheek against the top of his head. And it was a long time before either of them stopped crying.

Gregor's supper consisted entirely of raw fish as he gave his small ration of bread and meat to Boots. Temp, Howard, and Ares did the same, and she seemed satisfied. Giving a big yawn, she said, "We shut eyes?"

"Yeah, we shut eyes, Boots," Gregor said, and she snuggled up next to him on the floor.

Howard, ghost-white except for the purplish bruise that stained his jaw, insisted on steering so that Mareth could get some rest. Temp went on watch with Zap for light.

Before the rest went to sleep, Twitchtip spoke up. "We're getting close now. I can smell rats ahead."

"What of the serpents?" asked Mareth. "Do they still sleep?"

"Yes, but it won't be long before they surface. And they are deadly," said Twitchtip.

It really wasn't the last conversation Gregor wanted to hear before he went to bed. Rats . . . serpents . . . deadly . . . especially when he was already preoccupied by words like rager . . . killing . . . Bane. He could not get his mind to settle down. He went in and out of a sort of doze, never really losing consciousness, so he was the first one to rouse when Temp sounded the alarm.

"Going, the shiners are, gone!" he croaked.

Gregor sat up and opened his eyes and saw . . . nothing. It was pitch-black. He could hear Howard fumbling around behind him, muttering, "Conniving, vile creatures!"

He flipped on the flashlight he always kept right next to his bed. Everyone was stirring now.

"What is it? What has happened?" Mareth asked, springing to his feet.

"The shiners have deserted!" Howard said, getting a torch lit.

"Deserted? They were bound for the entire journey!" said Mareth.

"By what? Their honor? They have none. Their word? Equally worthless! The shiners are bound only by their stomachs, and as we cannot satisfy those, they have broken with us!" said Howard.

"But where could they go?" asked Gregor. It was days and days back to where they'd first hooked up with the bugs.

"They'll go to the rats," Twitchtip said flatly. "They'll receive food and safe passage home in exchange for information on our whereabouts." She looked around at their dismayed faces. "On the good side, we won't have to listen to them whine anymore."

For an instant, everyone else was too startled to speak. Twitchtip had made a joke! Then, everybody — humans, bats, roach, rat — laughed. If there was one thing they all could agree on, it was how annoying the fireflies had been.

"Yes," agreed Luxa. "That will be a blessing." She and Twitchtip eyed each other. "It is a shame you did not get to eat them, though."

"Oh, shiners taste nasty," said Twitchtip. "I only threatened them to shut them up."

"Well, no one shall miss them, but they have left us with more trouble," said Mareth. "How holds the fuel, Howard?"

Howard shook his head. "Not well. Much of it was in the other boat. We will get to the Labyrinth, but we will not have many more hours of light after that."

Light . . . life . . . the words were interchangeable to the humans down here.

"I have life — I mean, light! I have light, too!" said Gregor.

"You have the greatest task ahead of you, Overlander," said Howard. "You must keep your light."

"Well, I will, some of it. But I could spread it around. Wait a minute!" Gregor dumped out his bag. There were four flashlights, counting the one he slept with, plus his mini one from Mrs. Cormaci, and a lot of good batteries. He'd used the flashlights very sparingly on the trip since the fireflies were on. There was also that roll of duct tape.

"Hey, Luxa, give me your arm! Not the sword one!" he said. Luxa held out her arm curiously. Gregor placed a flashlight on her forearm so it would shine out over the top of her hand. Then he wrapped duct tape around and around, securing the flashlight to her sleeve, but leaving the on/off switch clear. "There! That way you won't have to hold it, and you won't lose it, either."

Luxa flipped the flashlight on and shone it about. "Oh, yes, Gregor. This will work well."

Gregor fixed up Howard and Mareth with flashlights, too, then attached one to his own arm. He had to use his sword arm, though, since the other was so wrecked from the squid.

There was a rustling, and a little hand reached up and patted his stomach. "Me, too, Ge-go. Boots have light, too!"

"Sorry, Boots, I'm out of flashlights. Oh, hang on," he said. He took the mini flashlight and taped it onto her sleeve.

Very pleased, Boots hurried over to the cockroach. "Boots have light, too, Temp!"

"Okay, but you've got to turn it off. Save the light, right?" Gregor said, flipping off her switch. He said it to Boots, but the others, who had also been flashing around their beams, guiltily turned them off. Gregor smiled. He could tell they all thought the flashlights were pretty cool.

He only had about six spare batteries. The Underlanders insisted that he keep them, and he didn't put up much of an argument. Howard was right about Gregor being the guy who had to take down the Bane, and that sure wasn't going to happen in the dark, with him relying on echolocation.

As Gregor was about to turn off his own flashlight, something caught his eye. For days they had been in a huge void, with no land in sight except for that deadly island. Now he could see towering rock walls flanking them on either side. They must be in some kind of channel.

Twitchtip's nose was going like crazy. "We will be there in minutes. And Photos Glow-Glow and Zap have done their work. The rats are waiting for us."

"Can you tell how many?" asked Luxa.

"Forty-seven," Twitchtip said without a pause. "They are waiting in the tunnels above the Tankard."

"What's the Tankard?" asked Gregor.

"It's a round, large shaft, very deep, half-filled with water. The serpents sleep on its floor," said Twitchtip.

"So, the serpents are some kind of fish?" said Gregor.

"No, they breathe air. But they can sleep under-water for long periods," said Howard.

Gregor thought of alligators. They could sleep under-water, too. He hoped these weren't giant alligators — the regular-sized ones were scary enough.

"I can smell it!" Twitchtip said. She rose up on her back feet, leaning her front feet on the bow. "I can smell the Bane!"

Up until that moment, Gregor had been secretly half-hoping they'd gotten the whole thing wrong. That maybe the Bane was like a fairy tale or a myth or something, and the rats had just been planting the rumor it was around. But if Twitchtip could smell it . . .

"Are you sure?" asked Gregor. "I mean, how do you know it's the Bane and not another rat?"

"I can smell its whiteness," said Twitchtip. "Only a flash, here and there. It's deep in the Labyrinth, and there are many layers of stone between us. But it's definitely there."

Gregor felt the need to move. He paced up and down the four-foot strip of floor that was available to him. "Okay, so what's the plan? I mean, what do we do when we get to this Tanker?"

"Tankard," said Howard. "There are several entrances to the Labyrinth in the tunnels above the Tankard. Our original plan involved secretly slipping into one of them and tracking down the Bane on foot. But this was before the shiners turned on us."

"So much for Plan A. What's Plan B?" asked Gregor. There was a long pause. "Come on, everybody has a Plan B!"

"In all fairness to the council, Overlander, coming up with any plan that brought us this far was difficult," said Mareth. "In the Underland, in the event that a plan fails, we usually have two options to fall back on: We may fight or flee."

"Flee?" Ahead lay rat-filled tunnels. Behind lay the Waterway with nowhere to land except that island teeming with flesh-eating insects. "There's nowhere to flee!" said Gregor.

"That makes our decision simpler," said Howard. He began to pass out swords.

"Twitchtip, which entrance betters our chance of survival?" asked Mareth.

"There's one at the far end of the Tankard. It's right at the waterline. No rat's been in it for years. It may be forgotten, or it may hold some danger that keeps the rats away from it, although I can't detect what that would be," said the rat.

"Can you direct us once we enter the Tankard?" asked Mareth.

"We are already here," said Twitchtip.

Gregor flipped on his flashlight, and the others followed suit. They were floating across what appeared to be a giant, round pool. The surface was as smooth and unbroken as a mirror. There were no beaches; the water went straight up to stone walls on all sides. Tunnel openings dotted the walls, some almost concealed by the waterline; others, hundreds of feet up. In many of them, Gregor could see a large rat.

No one moved. Not the rats. Not the visitors. An eerie silence surrounded them. Then there was a slight scraping sound from above.

Splash! Something landed off to their right, causing a fountain of water to spray into the air. Splash! Splash! The rats were tipping boulders out of the tunnels and sending them hurtling to the water below.

"Well, that's weak. None of the rocks are even getting near us," said Gregor. It was true; the boulders were missing them by a mile. He felt a little better, knowing the rats were launching such a worthless attack.

Splash! Splash! Splash! Splash! Splash!

Luxa frowned. "Something is wrong here."

Mareth nodded. "Yes, it is not like the gnawers to waste their energies on futile attacks."

Howard's eyes widened, and he began waving his arms frantically. "Get the boat up! Fliers! Get the boat up now!"

Twitchtip sprang up at almost the same time. "They're waking! They're waking! Fly!"

And that's when Gregor put it all together. The rats weren't trying to sink their boat with the rocks — they were trying to wake the serpents! Aurora and Andromeda latched on to the front ropes; Ares got his claws around the two loops in the back. They lifted the boat out of the water, spinning it in a circle as they rose.

"Where fly we?" came from all three bats.

"Twitchtip, where lies the tunnel?" asked Mareth.

"Stop spinning the boat so fast and I'll tell you!" said the rat. The bats maintained a slower circle, and Twitchtip indicated a tunnel opening opposite the channel they'd come in by. "There! The one shaped like an arch!"

Gregor caught it in his flashlight beam. It was only about six feet high, and you could've swum right into it. "But it's half under water! Does it even have a floor?"

"Further in. Look, this is no time to be picky," snapped Twitchtip. "The serpents are —!"

Bam! Something hit the side of the boat, ripping away a chunk of it. They were knocked sideways. The bats barely managed to hang on.

Gregor thought one of the rats' rocks had made contact. Then he saw it. "Oh!" he gasped. "Oh, geez!"

His first thought was, "So, I guess they're not extinct after all." He meant dinosaurs, but that wasn't quite right. Dinosaurs had the ability to walk on land. This creature propelled itself with flippers. Some kind of aquatic reptile then, but as old as the dinosaurs. And as big as the biggest skeletons he'd seen at the museum in New York City. Its body was a flattened oval. A whip-like tail beat the water, causing waves to roll across the calm pool. The neck was at least thirty feet long, and atop its sinuous, scaly pink length was a bullet-shaped head. There were indentations where eyes might have been, somewhere in its evolution, but they were long gone. What use were eyes to it down here? Its mouth opened, letting loose a low howl that chilled Gregor right down to his DNA. And then his light hit the teeth. Hundreds and hundreds of teeth in three rows headed their way. Crunch! Another piece of the boat was gone!

"Abandon ship!" Mareth choked out.

Gregor was impressed he'd managed to form a coherent sentence at all. He grabbed up Boots and his pack in one swoop and stumbled for Ares.

"On the count of three, everyone jumps!" called Mareth.

Gregor realized he meant "jumps off the side of the boat." It was the only way the bats could catch them. He scrambled up onto the edge.

"One — two — three!" Gregor felt his legs pushing off the boat, and then it was gone, but almost immediately Ares was under them. The bat dipped and swerved, and Temp landed behind them. The poor roach was shaking like a leaf. Well, who wasn't? Temp began nudging him in the back with his head. Gregor turned and saw the roach had a sword in his mouth.

"Oh, man, thanks, Temp!" Gregor said, grabbing the hilt with his good hand. He hadn't even thought to bring it. Some warrior.

Everyone's flashlight was on high beam now, which was good, since the single torch that had been lit had just hit the water with a sizzle. A prehistoric nightmare unfolded before them. Half a dozen serpents had broken the surface of the pool, and Gregor had a bad feeling that more were coming. They were swinging their heads and tails through the air, trying to take down whatever they could find. Since they had no eyes, Gregor guessed they had some other direction system. Maybe even echolocation.

There was no chance of fighting them. It was all Gregor could do to cling to Ares's back while the bat dodged the heads and tails frantically. He caught glimpses of Mareth and Howard on Andromeda, Luxa on Aurora . . . but wait a minute! Where was Twitchtip? Gregor heard a shriek and saw poor Twitchtip dangling by the tail from a serpent's mouth.

"Go, Ares!" he cried, and the bat flew straight for the rat. Gregor lifted his sword to attack when a tail caught Ares broadside and sent them hurtling into the air. Boots flew from his arms. "Boots! No!" he screamed. "Ares! Get her, Ares!" But the bat caught him first.

"Luxa has her!" the bat cried, before Gregor could flip out. "Luxa has her and Temp!"

"Get in the tunnels!" Howard shouted as Andromeda whizzed by. "The tunnels!" He was sitting upright on the bat, trying to hold on to an unconscious, bloody Mareth.

Twenty-foot-high waves were rolling across the pool now, smashing into the rock walls. Rats who had not moved quickly enough into their tunnels were screaming in the serpents' mouths. The air was filled with drench-ing splashes from the impact of the reptiles' tails.

Gregor felt Ares dive. They went straight into the waves, and for a moment he was submerged. When they came up, he was coughing and bewildered. He could feel his bat struggling under the weight of something. They rose in the air, jerking this way and that, as Ares dodged the numerous snapping mouths. Then the bat rocketed toward a stone wall, dipped, and they were inside a tunnel.

Ares dropped his burden and collapsed. Gregor rolled off his back and hit the floor with a thud. There was light behind them in the tunnel. Howard was rapidly working over Mareth on the ground, while Andromeda hung over them. One of Mareth's pant legs was soaked in blood. In front of him, Gregor saw the shuddering heap of wet fur that was Twitchtip. Blood poured from her nose, which appeared to have been smashed in, and oozed from the stump that had been her tail.

There was a sound at the front of the tunnel, and Gregor aimed his flashlight beam, hoping to see Aurora come in with Luxa, Boots, and Temp.

Instead, shooting down the tunnel at them were three rows of bared teeth.

CHAPTER

18

The sword Temp had saved was still in his hand. As the jaws were about to snap down on Twitchtip, Gregor vaulted over her and drove the blade straight down into the serpent's tongue. Liquid spurted up into his face. He stumbled back and slipped in a puddle of Twitchtip's blood. His feet went out from under him, and he landed against the rat's body.

The creature reared up, smashing its head into the tunnel ceiling. Rocks showered down on them. Gregor could physically feel the serpent's primeval roar going through him. It continued crashing its head up and down in pain and rage as it withdrew from the tunnel, the sword still lodged in its tongue.

Would more come in?

"I need another sword!" Gregor shouted, and Howard tossed one up to him. He stood crouched before Twitchtip, senses heightened. He could feel himself buzzing on the edge of going into that rager mode. He fought it, trying not to lose control as he stood there awaiting the next onslaught. It never came. Maybe word had gotten around that if you stuck your head down this tunnel you could mess up your tongue. Or maybe the serpents had found more interesting food. Whatever it was, things were beginning to quiet down out there. The howls became fewer, the splashes died.

Gregor unclenched his hands and turned around. Ares was right behind him, providing backup. Twitchtip had both paws on her nose to staunch the flow of blood. Howard was pounding on Mareth's chest, trying to restart his heart.

"Mareth!" Gregor ran back to where the soldier lay on the ground. "Come on, Mareth!"

Howard pounded a few more times and pressed his ear against Mareth's chest. "His heartbeat is back! What have you in your pack, Overlander?"

Gregor dumped his pack on the floor. It held his last batteries, the duct tape, the two candy bars, and a few catch cloths he'd put in to have handy in case Boots needed a change.

Howard ripped off the remains of Mareth's blood-soaked pant leg, revealing jagged flesh around a gaping wound. "A serpent bit him when we went to help Twitchtip." He laid three catch cloths over the wound. "Hold them," he ordered Gregor. Then he wrapped the duct tape around the leg to keep them in place. He sat back on his heels and shook his head. "We have to get him home, if he is to survive. Warm him, Andromeda, while I tend to the rat."

Andromeda lay beside Mareth and enfolded him in her wings. "I must take him home. I must take him home."

Howard grabbed the last two catch cloths and went to Twitchtip. He used one to bandage the stump of her tail. "I am sorry I had to sever it," he said to the rat. "There was no other way to free you."

"I would've bit through it myself if I could have," said Twitchtip.

Howard placed the other catch cloth over her nose and wound duct tape around it. "You will have to breathe through your mouth, until it heals." The rat nodded.

"What happened to your nose?" asked Gregor.

"Just before Howard cut me free, a serpent crushed it with his tail," said Twitchtip. "I can't smell a thing."

"You can't smell?" said Gregor. Twitchtip would not be able to smell the Bane then, but there was a much more pressing matter. "Then you can't tell, where my sister is, I mean?"

"Do not fret, Overlander. My cousin and Aurora are an excellent team. I am sure they have all taken refuge in one of the tunnels," said Howard. But he looked uneasy.

"I believe they meant to," Twitchtip said, avoiding Gregor's gaze.

Gregor felt time stop. "You believe they meant to?"

Twitchtip hesitated. "It was all very confusing. The serpent was swinging me around and there was so much motion, it was difficult to place any smell."

"Luxa and Aurora caught Boots. They caught Temp. Aurora said this to me," said Ares.

"Yes, they did. I know their smells were all together. But then . . . but then . . . there was water between us," said Twitchtip.

"What does that mean? There was water between us?" Gregor said.

"It means . . . I still smelled them. But there was water between us. Many feet of it. Their scent was getting fainter. And that's when the serpent hit my nose and everything went dark," said Twitchtip.

"You think . . . they were pulled under, then?" said Howard.

"I don't know for sure. But that would be my guess, if I were forced to make one," said Twitchtip. She looked up at Gregor. "I'm sorry, Overlander."

"This did not happen. I will call. I will call for Aurora now!" Ares said, and shot out of the tunnel.

No one moved while he was gone. Gregor's body was slowly turning to ice. The numbness started in his feet and began spreading up his legs. Over his hips. Up through his stomach. By the time Ares came back and landed beside him, it had reached his rib cage.

"There is no answer," said the bat.

And the ice encircled his heart.

DIE THE BABY, DIE HIS HEART,

DIE HIS MOST ESSENTIAL PART.

They had killed Boots. Nothing could be worse than this.

He imagined going back to New York City and walking in the front door of his apartment . . . alone.

"What do you wish to do, Gregor?" Howard asked, after some indistinguishable period of time had passed.

> *DIE THE BABY, DIE HIS HEART,*
> *DIE HIS MOST ESSENTIAL PART.*
> *DIE THE PEACE THAT RULES THE HOUR.*
> *GNAWERS HAVE THEIR KEY TO POWER.*

They were off celebrating somewhere, the gnawers. Gnashing their ratty teeth and laughing and congratulating one another on how well their plan had worked. On how they had killed his baby sister and broken him in two.

The ironic thing was that, for the first time, Gregor could envision what he was going to do.

"Gregor?" repeated Howard.

The ice had come up over his throat, and his voice was calm and cool. "I want you guys to go home. Get Mareth back. Twitchtip, too, if you can," said Gregor.

"And what will you do, Overlander?" asked Twitchtip.

Gregor felt the last bit of warmth disappear as the ice went across his forehead and up over the top of his head. There was nothing left that anyone could do to him now. There was nothing left to fear.

"Me?" he said. "I'm going to go kill the Bane."

PART 3

The Maze

CHAPTER

19

"You cannot. You cannot do it alone," Howard said, with a shake of his head.

"Yes, I can," said Gregor. "Tell them why, Twitchtip."

Twitchtip raised one rat eyebrow at Gregor, to see if he was sure. He nodded. "All right, then," she said. "He may stand a chance. He's a rager."

The word had an effect on everybody. Ares and Andromeda both ruffled their wings. Howard's mouth dropped open. "A rager?" he said. "How know you this?"

"Ragers put out a very specific scent when they fight," said Twitchtip. "It's slight, even for me, but I can detect it. I smelled it the first time I met the Overlander, but later wondered if I'd confused it with Ripred's scent. He'd been fighting as well."

"I was hitting the blood balls that day," said Gregor. "That was the first time I felt like that."

"Yes, and then when the squid attacked, I was certain about it," said Twitchtip. "I told him he was a rager a few days later, but he denied it."

There was a pause, and Gregor could feel the others watching him. "Because I didn't want it to be true. But that doesn't matter, what I want. I don't know what it is; something happens when I fight. Something weird. And if Twitchtip thinks she smells this rager thing on me, she's probably right."

"Well, say it is true, Gregor, and you are a rager. It does not make you immortal. It does not mean you can walk into a maze full of rats alone," said Howard.

"He will not be alone," said Ares. "I will be with him."

"And I'll lead him into the maze as far as I'm able," said Twitchtip. "I got a good whiff of white fur before I lost my nose. If I can't lead him to the Bane, I can get him close."

"Then Andromeda and I will come, too," said Howard.

"You're not invited," said Gregor.

"What?" said Howard.

"I don't want you in the maze, Howard. I want you to take Mareth back and tell people what happened. Someone has to. And if I don't come back, I need you to somehow get word to my family," said Gregor.

"You are not in charge of this mission," said Howard. "I had orders from Regalia."

"Okay, but if you try to follow me, I'll fight you," said Gregor.

"You will not stand a chance on foot, fighting a rager on a flier," said Ares.

"Especially with a rat on their side," threw in Twitchtip.

Howard was starting to lose it now. "Maybe I will take that chance! Maybe Andromeda will, too!"

"Please don't, Howard. Please go back. I don't want my mom and dad waiting for Boots and me to walk in the door when it's not going to happen. And sooner or later, if we don't show up, I know they'll come looking for us," said Gregor. "And they need to know in Regalia, too. About Luxa. They have to find a new queen or king now, right? Because no matter what Luxa said, Nerissa probably can't handle it. So it will be Vikus, then your mom, and then you. But if you die, it will be —"

"Stellovet. Oh, I did not think of that," said Howard.

"You going to leave her in charge of Regalia?" asked Gregor.

"No, I am not, I am —" Howard ground the palms of his hands into his forehead. Between losing Pandora and Luxa, whom he'd only just found, really, and the responsibility of a kingdom hanging over him — he was clearly overwhelmed. "I do not know what to do. Andromeda, what say you?"

"I will not fight the Overlander and risk injuring him. I am taking Mareth home," said Andromeda. "And you should come with me."

"Oh . . ." The resistance seemed to go out of Howard. "I cannot fight all of you," he said. He sat there for a few moments, his head bowed. Then he shook it off and tried to get back to business. "Well, then, every second counts if we hope to get Mareth back alive. But Andromeda cannot make the flight without rest, and there is nowhere safe to land."

That was true. They all pondered it, then Ares spoke up. "There are some pieces of the boat in the Tankard. Not large, but they still float."

"Maybe you could make them into a lifeboat," said Gregor.

"What is this, a lifeboat?" asked Howard.

"In the Overland, big boats, like ships and things, have lifeboats attached to them. They're small boats you can get in if your ship sinks or something," said Gregor.

"If the boat were light enough to carry, and I could rest for a few hours at times, I could make it," said Andromeda.

Ares volunteered to search for wreckage.

"I'll go with you," said Gregor. He needed to talk to his bat. He waited until they were flying out over the Tankard to speak. "You don't have to do this, Ares. Come after the Bane. I'll go alone."

"No. We will go together," said Ares. "Besides, the gnawers have killed every reason I had to return to Regalia. If by some strange chance we live and you return home, the silence begins for me."

What the bat said was true. With Luxa and Aurora gone, Ares would have no contact with anyone. He could probably sit in his hideout for years without anyone bothering to check on him. Gregor would go home, his heart dead, and Ares would be as good as banished.

"Okay," said Gregor. "We'll go together." He had a feeling they would never have a discussion like this again — about whether one would go into danger without the other. He didn't bother to thank Ares. Somehow they were past thanking each other. Somehow it would almost be like thanking himself. Gregor realized that the journey filled with squids and whirlpools and mites and serpents and loss, great loss, had changed them. It had made the oath they had sworn in front of that furious crowd in Regalia real. He remembered the feel of Ares's claw clasped in his hand and thought of the words he'd said with Luxa prompting him.

"ARES THE FLIER, I BOND TO YOU,
OUR LIFE AND DEATH ARE ONE, WE TWO.
IN DARK, IN FLAME, IN WAR, IN STRIFE,
I SAVE YOU AS I SAVE MY LIFE."

Ares was his bat. Gregor was Ares's human. They were truly bonded now.

If there was one positive note, they made a good haul. Ares found three pieces of the boat, and Howard was able to fashion them into a sort of raft using the last few strips of duct tape. It wasn't anything you'd want to try crossing the Waterway on, but when they went down and tested it, it held up under the combined weight of Gregor, Ares, and Howard.

"It should do for a few hours at a time," said Howard. "Long enough for Andromeda to sleep a bit."

Almost as important as the boat wreckage were the two packs they retrieved. They had washed up inside one of the tunnels when the waves were high. The first contained food. The second, to Howard's great relief, was his first aid kit.

"Oh, this! This is as good as light itself!" he said. He immediately opened the pack and began to work on everyone. He changed Mareth's and Twitchtip's bandages, dousing the wounds with medicine. He rewrapped Gregor's arm, which was actually showing some improvement, and dabbed Ares's mite bites with salve.

Howard insisted Gregor take the rest of the food, since Mareth couldn't eat, anyway, and he and Andromeda could live on raw fish. "And who knows what you will find in the Labyrinth?"

Gregor took Mareth's sword; Howard still had his own.

Finally, they divided up light. They had two working flashlights; Howard's had died during the serpent attack, and two had disappeared into the deep with Luxa and Boots. So, there was one flashlight per party, but Howard made Gregor take every spare battery. "Even with no light, Andromeda will get us home. You have many more difficulties with which to contend."

Gregor nodded. He put his candy bars, the food, and the spare batteries in one backpack. He wedged Mareth's sword between two straps. The flashlight was still taped onto his good arm.

Andromeda flattened out her back, and they laid Mareth on it. Howard tucked the spare blanket from his first aid kit around him. Then he swung his leg over the bat's neck. "Fly you high, Gregor the Overlander."

"Fly you high," said Gregor. Although "Been nice knowing you" seemed more appropriate. He didn't really expect to see Howard again.

Andromeda took off, snagging the raft in her claws as she left the tunnel. Almost immediately, they were lost from view.

Gregor, Ares, and Twitchtip turned and headed into the tunnel without a word.

CHAPTER

20

Guided by what she remembered of the Labyrinth before her nose was injured, Twitchtip led Gregor and Ares through the maze. Almost at once, the tunnel began to divide. Some paths led to intersections that branched off into four or five directions. Others twisted around like a corkscrew so that it took ten minutes to cover the distance you could've walked in one if the path had been straight. As they moved farther into the maze, the tunnels became even more unpredictable. A narrow passage they could barely squeeze through would suddenly open onto a huge cavern that in turn would lead to an obstacle course of boulders.

It was hardest on Ares, since most of the journey had to be made on foot. He hopped along, fluttering, taking tiny, rapid bat steps in the tighter passages and opening his wings with relief when they reached a larger space.

There were no rats. "They must have witnessed your sister's fate," said Twitchtip. "The gnawers think they have defeated you, and the Bane is safe. But eventually one will get your scent, and then the fight begins."

They drove themselves forward for about an hour, then stopped to catch their breath.

"You can remember all this? Just from what you smelled from the Tankard?" Gregor asked Twitchtip.

"Well, that, and the fact that I'm more familiar than most with the Labyrinth. I lived here for about a year after I was banished," panted Twitchtip. She was not doing well. The bandages on her nose and tail stump were soaked with blood, and her eyes had a hot, fevered look.

"I thought you lived in the Dead Land," said Gregor.

"Not at first. I hid in a cave down by the Tankard. The rats never came there because of the serpents. It wasn't ideal, but it offered more protection than the Dead Land. Then one day I dozed off gathering mushrooms and a patrol saw me. I had to run, and the only place left to go was the Dead Land," said

Twitchtip. "I didn't speak to a soul for years. Then I realized there was another rat around."

"Ripred," said Ares.

"He let me stay in his nest sometimes, if he was gone. You've been near there. It's where you first spoke to him," said Twitchtip. "Now he has a whole band of rats. But I can only stay, he says, if I help you find the Bane," said Twitchtip. "Otherwise, I'll be on my own again." This fear seemed to rouse her. "We have to keep moving."

As they took off again, Gregor found himself thinking of Ripred. Letting Twitchtip stay near him in the Dead Land, letting her use his nest and join his pack, these could almost seem like acts of kindness. But were they? Everything was conditional on Ripred getting something back from Twitchtip. Ripred knew he could use her and that incredible nose. Twitchtip was desperate to belong somewhere again. They had mutual need. Like Ripred and Gregor did. For Twitchtip, like Gregor, the question would be what would happen when that need ran out.

Or was he being too hard on Ripred? He seemed to be friends with Vikus and Solovet. There had been moments when Gregor thought he'd sensed a genuine compassion in the rat, behind the sarcasm and the snarls.

Maybe things were more complicated for ragers. They certainly were for Gregor.

Twitchtip began to stumble, and Gregor could see she was about to give out. She lost her footing one last time, fell on her belly, and did not get up. He squatted down beside her. Her breathing was rapid and shallow.

"I can't go on," she said. "It doesn't matter — I'm at the end of my scent map, anyway. Ahead, the path splits in three directions. Your guess is as good as mine," she said.

"Are we supposed to just leave you here?" said Gregor.

"I'll rest awhile. If the rats don't find me, I may be able to make my way back to my old cave. But, you . . . you have to move forward now. You are close to the Bane. I know it. The rats will smell you soon. Go . . . go . . . ," she gasped.

Gregor pulled out a hunk of meat and some stale bread for her. What was there to say? "Fly you high, Twitchtip."

She laughed, and blood dripped from the bandage on her nose. "You don't say that to rats."

"What do you say in a situation like this?" asked Gregor.

"Like this? Run like the river," said Twitchtip.

"Run like the river, Twitchtip," said Gregor.

"You, too," said Twitchtip.

And Gregor and Ares left her lying on the tunnel floor. When they came to the place where the tunnel split in three, they paused. Gregor had an image of Twitchtip, lying in the darkness, bleeding to death.

Ares read his thoughts. "She is strong and cunning, to have survived in the Dead Land on her own. And she has a place near enough to hide."

"I know," said Gregor.

"She loathes her life alone. Your killing the Bane is her only hope. If I were Twitchtip, I would not want you to come back," said Ares.

Gregor nodded and surveyed the tunnels. "Which one looks good to you?"

"The one on the left," said Ares.

They followed it for a while, hit another corkscrew, and somehow wound up back at the stop where the three tunnels met.

"On further reflection, I favor the right," said Ares.

They took the right tunnel and within five minutes

had reached a dead end and retraced their steps to the opening.

"I think you should choose," said Ares.

They headed down the middle tunnel and after about twenty minutes arrived in a large, circular cavern. It was almost perfectly cone-shaped, with the walls slanting up fifty feet to meet at a single point at the top. Around the base, at least a dozen tunnels led out from it like the spokes on a bicycle wheel.

"Oh, great," said Gregor. "Now which way?"

Ares had no idea. "But, Overlander, it has been many hours since we fed. If we are to continue, we must eat."

When had they last eaten? Gregor tried to think back — back through the time with Twitchtip, through the serpent attack, through the passage into the Tankard, through Temp's voice waking him, through the night to that evening when they were all together. He'd eaten a slab of raw fish and given Boots all his bread and meat.

"We shut eyes?" he heard her little voice say, and a hot pain stabbed him in the heart. He took a deep breath, pushed Boots out of his mind, and imagined the rats laughing. The ice sealed back over his chest.

"You're right. We have to eat," Gregor said, and opened the pack. They sat on the stone floor, choking down the dry food, washing it down with water from a leather bag that looked like a wineskin.

"There is something wrong about it. My still being alive," Ares said out of the gloom.

"How do you mean?" asked Gregor.

"When Henry and Luxa and Aurora are no longer. How many days ago was it that you first fell?" asked the bat.

"I don't know. Maybe five or six months," said Gregor.

"There was a match. Henry and I had scored seven times. A feast was planned that night for Nerissa's birthday. The rats seemed far away. And then you ran into the arena with your sister and the crawlers, and nothing has ever been the same. What happened to that world? How did it change so quickly?" said Ares.

Gregor knew what he meant. His world had completely transformed the night his dad disappeared. And it had never really been right since. "I don't know. But I can tell you this, that world — it's not ever coming back."

"I let my bond die. I am an outcast. Luxa and Aurora are gone. It seems a crime for me to be alive," said Ares.

"It wasn't your fault, Ares. Not any of it," said Gregor. "It's like Vikus said to me once, we just all got trapped in one of Sandwich's prophecies."

This did not seem to cheer Ares up much. For a while he was silent, then his black eyes caught and held Gregor's gaze. "Will it make us feel any better, do you think, to kill the Bane?"

"I don't know," said Gregor. "But I don't see how it could make us feel any worse."

Ares's head lifted sharply in a manner Gregor had begun to recognize.

"Rats?" Gregor asked.

"Two of them. Coming at a run," said Ares.

In seconds, Gregor was on Ares's back. The bat shot up into the cone, and they were circling as the rats ran in. There were two, as Ares had predicted, with mud-gray coats and gnashing teeth.

"There he is!" cried one rat.

"We were fools to leave him with Goldshard," said the other.

"That will be remedied as soon as these are dead!" growled the first.

Although Gregor was well out of range, the rats began to leap for him immediately. They could not reach him, but they prevented Ares from flying down low enough to escape through one of the tunnels. Eventually, Gregor would have to fight them, and it was best to do it now, before Ares tired or more rats showed up.

As he pulled the sword from the strap on his pack, the rager sensation began. He didn't fight it this time. The rats broke up into fragments in his vision, as if he were looking at their reflection in a shattered mirror, but only certain parts were lit. He caught glimpses of an eye, a spot under a raised paw, a neck . . . and somewhere in his brain, he understood that these were his targets.

"Now," said Gregor quietly. And Ares began to dive.

Gregor was almost within striking distance of one of the rats when something caused Ares to veer straight upward. A third rat with an unusual gold coat had bolted into the cone right beneath them.

"That makes three to fight," Gregor thought as Ares shot up and off to the side, but as the ground came back into view, he could see the gold rat tearing the throat out of one of his attackers. Then it spun around, blood flying from its muzzle, to face the other gray rat.

Gregor shook his head slightly, to clear it. What was going on?

"Don't be an idiot, Goldshard! He's come to kill the Bane!" snarled the gray rat.

"I would rather have the Bane dead than have it trust you," the gold rat hissed back. The rat's voice was slightly higher pitched, like Twitchtip's, and Gregor felt certain it was female.

"All you guarantee is your own death!" The gray rat crouched down to lunge.

"Someone will die, Snare, the question is who?" said Goldshard. As Snare sprang toward her, she went into action.

Gregor had never seen a full-scale rat fight before. Ripred had killed two rats in a tunnel en route to rescuing his dad, but they hadn't had time to fight back. Then the big, scarred rat had taken on some of King Gorger's soldiers. But Gregor hadn't witnessed it because he was busy leaping to what he had thought would be his death. Now he had a bird's-eye view.

When Goldshard had killed the first time, she'd had the element of surprise on her side. This time her opponent was on the offensive. And Snare, who Gregor was pretty sure was a male, was a lot bigger than she was.

The combat was vicious. The rats attacked each other in violent bursts. They'd circle for a minute, looking for an opening, then one of them would leap and there would be a blur of teeth and claws. As they pulled apart to circle again, both would have new wounds.

Snare lost an eye. Goldshard's ear dangled from a shred of fur. You could see the bone in Snare's shoulder. Goldshard's left front paw was snapped in two.

Finally, the gold rat came in on her opponent's blind side and locked her fangs on his neck. In the final throes of death, Snare got his hind feet between their bodies and slashed open the length of Goldshard's belly. She lost her grip, staggered back, and collapsed. Her intestines spilled out on the ground. The rats lay a few feet apart, eyes locked in hate, bodies helpless. With a terrible gurgling sound, Snare suffocated in his own blood.

Goldshard turned her gaze to Gregor. The look was pleading, and he was sure she wanted to say something to him. "Don't . . . ," she whispered. But before she could finish, her eyes glazed over, and she stopped moving.

"What just happened?" Gregor blurted out.

"I do not know," said Ares.

"Are they dead?" asked Gregor.

"Quite dead. All three of them," the bat replied. He coasted down to the ground, avoiding the pools of blood that were spreading out from the rats' bodies.

"Do you know who they are?" asked Gregor. "Did you recognize their names? Goldshard? Snare?"

"Not Goldshard," said Ares. "I have heard of Snare. He was one of Gorger's generals. He was out fighting the war when Gorger fell. He must have joined with the Bane then. It would make sense. Whoever is close to the Bane would have much power when he becomes king," said Ares.

Gregor hadn't spent much time thinking about the rats' political struggles, but now that he did, something seemed strange. "So why hasn't the Bane become king yet? You'd think a rat as big and strong as he is would have taken over by now," said Gregor. "What's he waiting for?"

"Even the Bane must gather an army around him," said Ares. "He has his own enemies among the rats. Ripred, for instance. He wants the Bane dead."

That was true. Part of Ripred's plan for his own rise to power included killing the Bane. Snare had wanted to keep the Bane alive, but Goldshard was willing to let Gregor kill it rather than let it trust Snare.

There was something else about Goldshard. That last look she had given him. Like she was begging him, almost. What was it the rat had wanted to say to him? Don't? Don't what? Hurt her? It was a little too late for that.

Ares's head snapped around to a tunnel entrance.

"How many?" asked Gregor.

"Just one, I think," said Ares. "It is hard to tell. The path spirals." His chin jerked up again. This time, Gregor did not have to ask; he had heard the scratching himself. The sound stopped. Nothing emerged from the tunnel. Suddenly Gregor knew why.

"It's the Bane," he whispered to Ares. The bat gave a nod of agreement. It had to be. The other rats would simply attack, but the Bane knew it was being hunted. By a human. By an Overlander. By the warrior.

The words of "The Prophecy of Bane" came back to Gregor.

HEAR IT SCRATCHING DOWN BELOW,

RAT OF LONG-FORGOTTEN SNOW,

EVIL CLOAKED IN COAT OF WHITE

WILL THE WARRIOR DRAIN YOUR LIGHT?

Yes, he would. That was what the warrior had come to do.

There was another faint scratch. It was in there then. Just a few feet away. Waiting.

The tunnel mouth was small, only about five feet

high and four feet wide. There would be no flying in on Ares. The Bane must know that. It wanted to lure him in alone. Okay, then. He'd face it alone.

Gregor slid the pack off his shoulders and onto the ground. He didn't want anything restricting his movements. He checked the switch on his flashlight; it was already on high beam. Gripping his sword, he began to move toward the tunnel.

Ares's wing came up to stop him. "You cannot fight him in there, Overlander."

"Well, he's not coming out," said Gregor.

"Wait, then," said Ares.

"For what? Another bunch of rats to show up?" said Gregor.

Ares dropped his wing reluctantly.

"Look, I've got a feeling it was supposed to be this way, anyway. Like I was supposed to do it alone," said Gregor. "But you be ready, because after I kill it, we've got to get out of here fast. Okay?"

"I will be ready," said Ares. He extended his claw, and Gregor grasped it with his hand.

Then Gregor turned to the tunnel. In the dozen paces it took him to reach the opening, he could feel himself slipping into rager mode, the heightened senses, the rush of adrenaline, the selective vision. Every molecule in his body was preparing to kill.

He moved swiftly inside and almost immediately encountered the spiral Ares had mentioned. Another corkscrew-like path. With his bad hand tracking along the wall and his good one leading with his sword, he went around one, two, three full turns and burst out into a square chamber.

It was trying to hide from him, the Bane. He caught just a glimpse of white fur, a flash of pink tail in a cave off to the side of the chamber.

Gregor thought of Luxa, who would never be queen, of Twitchtip bleeding on the ground, of his dad crying on the phone, and of Boots . . . sweet, trusting Boots . . .

Heart pounding, blind to everything except that patch of fur, he lunged toward the cave. He raised the hilt in the air, flipping the sword so it would come down point first, at an angle. His bad hand joined his good one, and with every ounce of strength he drove the blade toward the Bane.

But just before the point made contact, the creature made a sound that hit Gregor like a cannonball.

"Ma-maa!"

CHAPTER

22

Gregor turned the sword at the last second, driving it into the stone wall of the cave with such force that the blade snapped off near the hilt and clattered to the floor. His teeth rattled at the impact.

He fell back from the cave. "Boots?" he said hoarsely. But he knew it wasn't Boots's voice. There'd just been something in it that was so like how Boots had sounded when she was upset, the pitch, the distress, and the way she'd break that word into two long syllables. *"Ma-maa!"*

The chamber reeled around his head. Where was the Bane? What was that white furry thing a few yards away? Because it sure wasn't some ten-foot rat trying to attack him!

Gregor forced himself forward and shone the flashlight into the cave. Huddled against the wall, shaking in fear, was a small, white rat. Suddenly it all made sense to him — why almost nothing was known about the Bane, why it had not taken over the rat kingdom, why it had not attacked him. It was only a baby!

Still, it was the Bane. He was supposed to drain its light. His blade had broken off, leaving a jagged daggerlike weapon in his hand. It would be so easy to kill the creature in front of him. But . . . but . . .

"Ma-maa!"

But it sounded just like Boots!

"Oh, geez. Oh, geez," Gregor said, and tossed aside what remained of his sword. He knelt down and reached out his hand to pat the thing. "It's okay. You're okay, baby."

The rat shuddered in terror and pressed back against the wall, wailing its head off. *"Ma-maa! Ma-maa!"*

"Shh! Shh! It's okay. I'm not going to hurt you," Gregor said soothingly. "Ares!"

He shouldn't have shouted. He'd scared it again, and now it was sobbing.

Ares scampered out of the last curve and wobbled into the chamber. "What is it? Where is the Bane?"

"In here," Gregor said, gesturing to the cave. "And we've got a problem."

"What? What?" Ares had come in ready to fight to the death, and now he was completely disoriented. "What is the problem?"

"This is the problem," said Gregor. He leaned down and scooped up the baby rat in his arms. It weighed about as much as a full-grown cocker spaniel. One day it probably would be ten feet tall. But today, he could pick it up and rock it. He turned to show Ares.

"What is that? That is not the Bane!" said Ares.

"Actually, I think it is. Or at least, it's a baby Bane," said Gregor.

"I do not believe it! That is some decoy. Some trick of the gnawers to lure us into a trap so that they may destroy us!" said Ares.

"I don't think so. I mean, look at its coat. How many white rats have you ever seen?" asked Gregor.

"None. Save this," said Ares. "But perhaps it is not a rat! Perhaps it is a mouse they have captured and used to deceive us! I have seen white mice!"

Gregor examined the baby, but he was no rodent expert. He held it up for Ares to inspect. "You take a look. Is it a mouse?"

"No. It is most definitely a gnawer," said Ares.

"So, you think there are two white rats?" said Gregor.

"Yes. No. I do not know. Two white rats at one time, it is highly improbable. It must be the Bane. Ohhh. Oh, Overlander. What are you going to do with it?" said Ares.

"Well, I can't kill it, can I? I mean, it's just a baby!" said Gregor.

"Aha! I doubt that argument will hold much water in Regalia!" said Ares. Gregor had never seen him off-balance. The bat was fluttering around the chamber, so agitated that he bumped into a wall.

"Hey, you bumped into something!" said Gregor. The bats never bumped into anything.

"Can you blame me? I am . . . we are . . . do you have any idea what you hold in your arms?" said Ares.

"The Bane, I guess," said Gregor.

"Yes! Yes! The Bane! The scourge of the Underland! The creature who may well cause the extinction of fliers, humans, and countless others. What we do at this moment determines the fate of all who call the Underland home!" said Ares.

"What am I supposed to do, Ares? Run my sword through its head? Look at the thing!" The Bane wiggled out of his arms and ran for the tunnel. "Hey! Wait a minute! Hold on, you!"

Gregor chased the baby rat through the corkscrew curves and out of the tunnel. What he saw made his heart ache.

The little white rat was trying to curl up in the curve of Goldshard's neck. *"Ma-maa,"* it whimpered. *"Ma-maa."* Getting no response, it pawed frantically at the dead rat's face. *"Ma-maa!"*

He heard the rustle of Ares's wings behind him. "So, that's it. She was its mom. And when she said 'Don't' to me . . ." Gregor had to stop for a minute. "She was trying to say, 'Don't kill my baby.'"

"She must have been desperate to keep it from Snare. He would have taken the pup and raised it to do his bidding," Ares said quietly.

Blood was staining the baby's white fur. Its cries were piteous. As if that wasn't enough to deal with, Ares's head whipped up.

"How many this time?" asked Gregor.

"A dozen, at least," said Ares. "You must decide what to do, Overlander."

Gregor bit his lip. He couldn't decide. Everything was happening too fast. He needed more time. "Okay, okay," he said. He bounded over and lifted the baby into his arms. "We're taking it with us."

"We are?" Ares said, as if the thought had never crossed his mind.

"Yeah. Because I'm not going to kill it, and I'm not leaving it here for the other rats to use," said Gregor.

Ares shook his head in a combination of exasperation and denial, but he offered his back.

Gregor grabbed his backpack in one hand, threw a leg over Ares, and settled the Bane in front of him. "Okay," he said. "Let's run like the river."

As Ares lifted into the air, a dozen rats galloped into the cone. They took in the dead bodies, the bat, the baby in Gregor's arms.

"The Overlander has the Bane!" shouted one, and the whole pack went wild, howling, leaping into the air, slashing at the invaders with their claws.

"Hold on!" said Ares. Of the dozen tunnels that led out of the cone, about four were big enough for Ares to fly down. He dove for one, and they were off.

It was like the most horrifying theme park ride ever. Gregor hated those rides, but they were nothing compared to this spinning, jerking, flipping around in the dark, with only his flashlight beam, and insane live rats jumping out at him from every turn. Gregor clung to Ares with his legs and one hand while he kept the other arm wrapped around the baby.

At one point, when they were darting around a cave barely evading several sets of snapping teeth, Ares cried out, "Use your sword!"

"I don't have it! It broke and I left it back in the cave!" said Gregor. He hated dumping this whole escape thing on Ares, but what could he do?

Ares twisted sideways and made it into a tunnel with the rats hot on his tail.

The baby rat had given up crying *"Ma-maa!!"* and was now issuing a series of high-pitched alarm shrieks. "Eek! Eek! Eek!"

"Make it stop, Overlander. Its voice carries great distances. Every rat in the maze can hear that the pup is threatened!" shouted Ares.

Gregor remembered how far Boots's cry carried — through doors, down hallways, you could even hear her on the elevator when you were coming up. It was like nature had designed her baby cry so it would travel. Must be the same with rats.

At first he tried to calm the Bane with his voice. It wasn't enough. It might have helped if they were sitting somewhere quietly on the ground, but it was useless here in this nightmare of motion. He tried stroking its back and head, but that didn't work, either. Gregor's human voice and touch and smell were just more scary unknown things to the rat. Finally he managed to get a hand into his backpack and pull out one of the candy bars. He ripped it open, broke off a piece, and stuck it into the baby's wailing mouth.

There was an "Eek!" of surprise, then a smacking sound, and the Bane was consumed by its first wonderful taste of chocolate.

"More!" It was so weird to hear the rat baby talking, but it was. "More!" it said again, just like Boots would have.

Gregor popped another piece of chocolate into the little rat's mouth, and it was gobbled up. The Bane seemed to think better of him now that he had given it chocolate. It relaxed a little, back into his body, which made it easier to hold on to.

"You think we're almost out of here?" Gregor said as they swept out of a tunnel.

"See for yourself," said Ares.

Gregor shone the flashlight around the place they'd just entered. Lying on the floor were Goldshard, Snare, and the third rat. "No! What are we doing back here?" he gasped.

"Perhaps you should try navigating!" said Ares. What with him insisting on taking the Bane, having no sword, and being pretty worthless in general at the moment, Gregor could tell the bat had lost patience with him.

"Okay, okay, I'm sorry," said Gregor.

"It is our scent, Overlander," said Ares. "They track us with such ease. I cannot lose them."

"Hey, I know!" said Gregor. "Maybe we can trick them!" He'd seen some movie once where a guy running from bloodhounds had fooled them. "We need to confuse their noses." But with what?

Gregor ripped the bandage from his arm. It was soaked with blood and pus and ointment. "Fly around the cone, Ares! I need to touch the top of every tunnel."

Ares followed his instructions, if not his plan. "Why do we do this?"

Gregor held out the bandage and swiped it along the inside of every tunnel entrance as they passed it. "I'm just trying to spread our scent around."

They completed the full circle, hitting each tunnel opening. Gregor tossed the bandage up the last one.

"They come!" warned Ares.

"Get out! Get out now!" said Gregor.

Ares dipped into a tunnel they had not yet tried. After about thirty seconds, they could hear the rats reaching the cone. And they *were* confused. Different rats were calling for them to chase down different tunnels. A big argument broke out, and then the sound of fighting.

It grew softer as they moved away, until Gregor could no longer hear it at all.

Ares zigzagged down a tunnel, and this one opened out over a nice, wide, shallow stream.

"I must stop for a moment . . . I must drink . . ." Ares landed on the edge of the stream, panting. He dunked his face in the water, gulping it down.

Gregor got down and scooped up handfuls of water for himself and the Bane. The stream was not too deep, but the current was fairly strong and he didn't want the baby being swept away.

Ares raised his wet face. "I have only just thought of something," said Ares. "This stream. Where do you suppose it goes?"

"I don't know. A bigger stream. Maybe a river eventually, or —" Gregor caught Ares's drift. On his very first night in Regalia, when he'd tried to escape, he'd followed the water out of the palace. It had led to a river that had led to the Waterway. "It's sure worth a try."

Gregor hauled the Bane onto Ares's back, and they took off again.

It was not too promising for a while. The main thing about the stream was that it was long and it had as many twists and turns as the tunnels in the maze. Gregor could feel Ares's wings slowing; he was going to have to have a real rest soon. But to stop in the maze was certain death. The rats would catch up to them. Gregor had no sword. The baby would begin to cry again, and then they would —

"A river," Ares puffed out. "A river is at hand."

In another minute, they followed the stream out of the tunnel and into a huge cavern. A river ran through it. They were out of the maze!

Ares flew up high above the water. There were stony cliffs along the sides.

"Any rats around?" asked Gregor.

"Just the one on my back," said Ares.

"You want to pull over and take a break?" said Gregor.

"In a short while. I want to put more distance between the gnawers and us. They will be coming, Overlander. We have the Bane," said Ares.

"Yeah, I bet they hate that," said Gregor. He petted the Bane's head. It was getting used to him now. It curled up against him and gave a big yawn. "You've had a pretty big day, huh, little guy?" It didn't take long for it to fall asleep.

They flew awhile in silence. Then Ares spoke in an odd voice. "Overlander, I think I know this place. I think we both do."

"What?" said Gregor. How could he possibly know where they were?

"Shine your light down," said Ares.

Gregor obeyed. There below them was the river, very wide now, and very strong. Hanging down from the high banks on either side of it were the remnants of a broken bridge.

"Oh," said Gregor. And the memory of that day flashed before his eyes. Running across the bridge, trying to go back for Boots, Ripred carrying him by his backpack as the bridge swung dizzyingly below, being smacked to the ground by Ripred's tail while the rat and Luxa and Henry and Gox had hacked away at the ropes that held the bridge and the pack of rats catching up to the cockroaches and his baby sister and — and —

It was the place where Tick had died.

"You're right," said Gregor. "How did we end up here, do you think?"

"The Tankard, the Labyrinth, and what remains of this bridge are all in the rats' domain," said Ares. "At least now we have some sense of where we are."

The bat coasted in and landed on the riverbank across from where the bridge had been hacked off. "It will be safer on this side. The rats would have great difficulty swimming the river, which is, as we know, filled with flesh-eating fish."

Gregor climbed off Ares's back holding the Bane, who was snoring softly. They were at the mouth of a tunnel. He ran his flashlight beam over the surrounding rocks, remembering how they'd been filled with waiting rats on their first visit. Now the rocks were empty. "Anything in the tunnel?" he asked Ares.

The bat shook his head. "Not as far as I can tell. I believe we are safe for the moment. Overlander, I must rest."

He could see Ares's weary eyes starting to shut. "You go ahead and sleep. I'll keep watch," he said. "And, Ares? You were amazing back there."

"I was not bad," Ares agreed, and promptly fell asleep, his back to the tunnel wall.

Gregor trained his flashlight down the tunnel. If any intruders appeared, he would be ready. He sat cross-legged on the ground with the Bane on his lap. The baby stirred restlessly in its sleep, probably reliving the trauma of the last few hours. He patted its back to quiet it. The Bane's fur was stiff with its mother's dried blood.

The baby snuggled closer to him. It was so much like holding Boots. Boots. Why wasn't he crying about her? He had cried for a roach, in a cave just across the river there, but hadn't shed one tear for his sister. He remembered how Luxa had told him, in that same cave, that she hadn't cried since her parents died. It had been that bad. Maybe something like that was happening to Gregor.

His fingers traced the outline of one of the baby's soft ears.

So it turned out Sandwich had been right again. The rats had killed Boots, and he could not kill the

Bane. Although, Gregor didn't think he could have killed the Bane even if Boots had survived. Or could he have? If he had thought that only one of them could live? He didn't know. But it didn't matter anymore.

"Now what?" he thought. "Now what?" He had to think clearly. He had to figure out what to do with the Bane.

He couldn't take it back to the rats' land. Goldshard had lost her life trying to protect it from her fellow rats. If he showed up with it in Regalia, he bet the humans would decide to kill it. If they let it live, which seemed unlikely, the rats would definitely overrun the city trying to get it back. For a brief moment he wondered if he could take it home with him, but he knew his mom wouldn't have any part in raising a ten-foot rat, especially when Boots had —

Okay, so what did that leave? Nothing, pretty much.

He looked out over the water.

This was such a sad place. Not just because of Tick, but because when he'd come through here on the first quest, he'd been in a party of ten, and of that ten, how many were still alive? He did the math in his head. Three. Only three. Tick had died here. Henry and Gox were lost when they rescued his father. Luxa, Aurora,

243

Temp, and precious Boots drowned at the Tankard. The only ones left alive were he and Ares and Ripred.

Ripred. He was going to go crazy when he found out Gregor hadn't killed the Bane. He wanted the Bane dead. That's why he'd brought Twitchtip and tried to teach Gregor echolocation. But then Ripred hadn't known the Bane was a baby, either. Would that make any difference to the rat? Maybe, just maybe, it would.

Gregor felt a plan beginning to form in his head.

Ares awoke after about three hours, famished. He went down to the river and came back with a large fish, not one of the flesh-eating kind. The Bane awoke and wolfed down fish with the bat while Gregor scraped the mold off a piece of cheese and finished the last of the bread.

While they ate, he bounced his plan off Ares. "Okay, I have an idea about what to do with the Bane."

"I am listening," said Ares.

"This tunnel, it leads back to Ripred's nest," said Gregor.

"Does it?" said Ares.

"Yeah, remember? Twitchtip said his nest was where we first met him. And we first met him at the other end of this tunnel," said Gregor.

"Oh, yes, after we had fought the spinners," said Ares.

"Right, so I say we go find Ripred and give him the Bane and let him deal with it," said Gregor. Ares opened his mouth to object, but Gregor held up his hand. "Wait! Only tell me why we can't do it if you can come up with a better plan."

There was a very, very long pause. "I do not have a better plan, but this one has no possible good endings," said Ares.

"Probably not," said Gregor. "So, should we give it a try?"

res insisted Gregor sleep for a few hours. When he woke, they began their trek into the tunnel. It was narrow initially, but soon opened up into a space wide enough for Ares to fly, which was a relief, since Gregor's arms were aching from carrying the Bane.

They stopped to break for a drink at a stream in a cavern.

"Remember you this place?" asked Ares.

"No," said Gregor. "Wait, maybe . . ." They had stopped here to rest when Ripred was their guide. "Is this where Henry tried to kill Ripred in his sleep?"

"Yes, and you stepped between them," said Ares.

"I couldn't figure out if you knew Henry was going to try to kill him," said Gregor.

"I did not. It was one of many things Henry neglected to mention to me," said Ares. Gregor could tell he didn't want to talk about it anymore.

As they flew on, the Bane began to whimper for its mother again. How bizarre this must all seem to the baby rat. Flying through the air on a bat, being held by a human, knowing something very wrong had happened to its mother. Gregor fed it the rest of the chocolate bar from the Labyrinth. He had one left but decided to save it for a real emergency.

The smell of rotten eggs began to permeate the tunnel, and Gregor knew that they were fast approaching the cavern where they had first encountered the spiders, Treflex and Gox. Ares landed at the entrance, and they went in on foot. The sulfur-scented water still rained down the walls. There, on the floor, was the husk of Treflex's body, all that remained of the spider after his companion, Gox, had drained his insides.

"Want to rest?" asked Gregor.

"Not here," said Ares.

"Good," Gregor said, even though what lay ahead was nasty.

The tunnel dripped the evil-smelling water down on them. Ripred had taken them through it with the idea of concealing their scent from the rats, and they had certainly reeked of rotten eggs when they came out. This trip was, if possible, less comfortable. Gregor had been wearing a hard hat the first trip, which had offered some protection. He had not been injured. He had been eager to find his father instead of dreading the moment when they next met. And he had been carrying Boots on his back, not a rat in his arms.

Poor Ares had ridden on Temp's back before, because the tunnel was so narrow and long. Now he limped along, scraping his wings on stone outcroppings, ducking his head in the eye-stinging drizzle.

In minutes, they were all soaked. The rat mewed miserably. Gregor trudged along, putting one foot in front of the other. He and Ares did not speak the entire time they were in the tunnel, although it was many hours.

When eventually they staggered out of the mouth into open space, Gregor's knees gave way under him and he sat on the ground hard. He expected the Bane, who'd been squirming for most of the trip, to try to run off. Instead, it burrowed up under his shirt and pressed against his chest.

Ares slumped against a rock next to him.

"Are there rats around?" asked Gregor.

"About ten are coming now. But that is what we want, right?" said Ares.

"That is what we want," said Gregor.

Neither of them made any attempt to move as the rats surrounded them. And then, he saw the diagonal scar that split Ripred's face.

"If I had known that you were coming, I'd have fixed the place up," said Ripred.

"Don't bother. We won't be here long. I just came to give you a present," said Gregor.

"For me? You shouldn't have," said Ripred.

"You brought me Twitchtip," said Gregor.

"Not because I expected anything in return," said Ripred. His nose was beginning to move; his eyes fastened on the lump under Gregor's shirt.

"You're getting something, anyway," Gregor said, and pulled up his shirt. The Bane slid out on the floor in front of him. Every rat except Ripred gasped. Seeing another rat, the baby started to run to Ripred, but it jumped back at the violent hiss that issued from his mouth and scurried over to Ares.

"You don't like little kids, do you?" said Gregor. Ripred had hissed at Boots, too.

"Not this one in particular," snarled Ripred. "What's it doing here?"

"I didn't know where else to take it," said Gregor.

"You were supposed to kill it!" said Ripred.

"But I didn't. I brought it to you," said Gregor.

"And what makes you think I won't kill it?" said Ripred.

"I don't think you'd kill a pup," said Gregor.

"Ha!" Ripred said, pacing angrily in a circle. Gregor wasn't sure whether that meant yes or no.

"Okay, how about I don't think you'd kill the Bane? Because if you do, you'll never get the other rats to follow you," said Gregor.

It was lucky he'd been sitting down, because Gregor smacked back onto the rock so fast, he would have cracked his skull open if he'd been standing up. As it was, it hurt plenty.

Ripred pinned him to the ground with one paw as he bared his fangs in Gregor's face. "And have you also thought that, under the circumstances, I might very well kill you?"

Gregor swallowed hard. The answer was yes. But instead of admitting it, he looked Ripred dead in the eye and said, "Okay, but I think I'd better warn you that, if we fight, you've only got a fifty-fifty chance of winning."

"I do?" said Ripred. It was enough to distract him for a second. "And why is that?"

"Because I'm a rager, too," said Gregor.

Ripred began to laugh so hard he fell over on his side. The other rats were laughing, too. Gregor didn't even feel like sitting up. "It's true," he said to the ceiling. "Twitchtip smelled it on me. Ask Ares."

No one asked Ares; they were guffawing too hard. That was one thing you had to give the rats: They enjoyed a good joke. Finally Ripred pulled himself together and swept his tail around, shooing the other rats away. "Go," he said. "Leave them to me."

"All right, Rager," he said when they were gone. "Tell me what happened, and don't leave out any details. I left you after our sorry excuse for an echolocation lesson *and* —"

"And then I ran into Nerissa," said Gregor. He told Ripred everything: about the fireflies and squid tentacles, about saving Twitchtip at the whirlpool and losing Pandora at the island, about the serpents in the Tankard and taking refuge in the cave. And then he found he couldn't go on.

"Yes, you six were in the cave and what about the others?" asked Ripred.

"They were lost," Ares said, after it was clear Gregor wasn't going to answer. And the bat picked up the story, telling how the remaining group had split. How Twitchtip had led them until she'd collapsed. How Goldshard and Snare had fought. How Gregor had taken the Bane. "And now we are here."

Ripred looked at them thoughtfully. "So, you are. What's left of you," he said. "I am sorry for your losses."

That was the thing about Ripred: One minute he was about to kill you, and the next he seemed to understand it was all you could do not to curl up into a ball and die.

"Just out of curiosity, Gregor, what do you expect me to do with that pup if I don't kill it?" said Ripred.

"I thought you might, you know, kind of raise it. Everyone's so afraid of what it's going to turn into. And if Snare had got hold of it, it probably would've grown up to be a monster. But maybe if you take care of it and stuff, it might turn out okay," said Gregor.

"You thought I'd be its daddy?" said Ripred, as if he hadn't heard right.

"Or, at least its teacher. One of the other rats could be its parent," said Gregor. "Just for, you know, eighteen years, or whatever."

"Ah, here's something you obviously don't know about rats," said Ripred. "That ball of fluff over there will be full grown by the time you've seen another winter."

"But . . . it's just a baby," said Gregor.

"Only humans grow so slowly," said Ares. "It is one of their great weaknesses. The rest of us in the Underland mature as the rats do. Some even more quickly."

"But how do you teach it everything it has to know?" said Gregor.

"Rats learn faster than humans. And what does it really need to know? To eat, to fight, to find a mate, to hate everyone who is not a rat. It doesn't take long to learn these things," said Ripred.

"You know other things," said Gregor. "About what goes on in the Overland, even."

"Well, I've spent a lot of time in your libraries at night," said Ripred.

"You come up and read books?" asked Gregor.

"Read them, eat them, whatever mood strikes me," he said. "All right, Overlander, you may leave the pup with me. I won't kill it, but I can't promise I can teach it much. And you know, there will be hell to pay in Regalia."

"I don't care," said Gregor. "If they think I'm going to do their dirty work, they can think again."

"That's the stuff, Boy. You're a rager. Don't let them push you around," said Ripred.

"I *am* a rager," said Gregor sheepishly.

"I know. It's just that there are brand-new ragers, and there are old veteran ragers who have fought in countless wars. And you would be . . . ?" said Ripred.

"The first kind," said Gregor. "And I don't even have a sword."

"How's your echolocation coming along?" asked Ripred.

"It's not," said Gregor. "I stink at it."

"But you'll keep practicing, because you have such unflagging confidence in my judgment," said Ripred.

"Okay, Ripred," Gregor said, too tired to get into an argument about the whole worthless echolocation thing. He stood up. "Are you going to be able to handle it? The Bane, I mean?"

"If it's anything like its mother, I'll have my paws full," said Ripred. "But I'll manage."

Gregor went over and patted the baby on the head. "You take care, you hear?" The Bane nuzzled his hand.

"Give it this, when we're gone," Gregor said, handing Ripred the remaining candy bar. "It'll help. Ready, Ares?"

Ares fluttered forward, and Gregor climbed on his back. "Oh, yeah, and about Twitchtip. You'll let her stay if she makes it back, right?"

"Oh, dear. You haven't become attached to Twitchtip, have you?" said Ripred.

"As rats go, she is among our favorites," said Ares.

Ripred grinned. "She can stay if she can drag her pathetic hide back here. Fly you high, you two."

"Run like the river, Ripred," said Gregor.

As they flew off, he looked back over his shoulder. The Bane was sitting next to Ripred, eating the candy bar, paper and all.

Maybe it would work out in the end.

CHAPTER

24

After they had flown for a while, Gregor remembered that Ares hadn't rested after the long trip through the tunnel. "You want to find a place and take a nap?" he asked. "I can keep watch." But even as he spoke, he yawned. He hadn't had much sleep, either.

"I am strangely wakeful," said Ares. "Why do you not sleep while we fly? I will rouse you when I have need of rest."

"Okay, thanks." Gregor stretched out on Ares's back. The fur was damp, and it smelled of rotten eggs, but Gregor's clothes were in no better condition. Beneath the fur was the warmth of Ares's body. He closed his eyes and let oblivion take over.

Ares let him sleep about six hours before waking him. They camped in a niche high in the rocks of a cavern. The bat conked out immediately after providing Gregor with a few raw fish.

Gregor picked up one of the fish and ripped off a strip of skin with his teeth. Then he took a bite of the cold meat. Howard had always cleaned the fish with a knife, cutting neat pieces away from the bones. Gregor didn't have a knife or even a sword now. And what did it matter, anyway? Still, hunched over his fish on the stone ledge, he felt like he was in a time warp. He'd become a Neanderthal man or something, tearing into raw flesh, just trying to get the life-sustaining calories into his body. That must have been a hard life. Of course, his own wasn't exactly a picnic.

He thought longingly of rich, fatty foods. Mrs. Cormaci's lasagna, loaded with cheese and sauce and noodles. Chocolate cake with thick frosting. Mashed potatoes and gravy. He ripped off a stubborn piece of fish with a grunt. It didn't take long, he thought, to erase hundreds of thousands of years of change if you were hungry.

Gregor wiped his hands on his pants and leaned back against the stone. He found himself staring into his flashlight beam, drawn toward the one bit of light in this huge, dark place. He was down to his last set of batteries. If they ran out, he'd be entirely dependent on Ares to get him out. Who was he kidding? He was already entirely dependent on the bat. In fact, it didn't really seem fair. Ares kept them alive about ninety percent of the time, anyway. Gregor didn't feel like he'd really been holding up his end of this bond thing.

"So, stop staring at your flashlight and keep an eye out for trouble!" he thought. Disgusted with himself, he swept the beam over the surrounding rocks. Nothing new. Still, he had to get better about being on watch. Howard had said there were tricks to keeping your mind alert. Gregor did his multiplication tables for a while; that seemed to help. Next he tried to remember the capitals of all fifty states. But that only lasted for, well, fifty states. Finally, he forced himself to calculate something he'd been consciously ignoring: the number of days he'd been in the Underland.

It was almost impossible to figure out. He'd been in Regalia less than two days before they'd set sail on the Waterway, he was pretty sure of that. He thought someone had said the trip to the Labyrinth was about five days. Then another day or two until he met up with Ripred? Nine days? Ten?

His family must be a complete wreck. He would be

coming home right around Christmas. Without Boots. Forever.

Gregor went back to his multiplication tables.

When Ares woke up, there was more raw fish and then they took off again. They followed the same pattern for a day or two. Gregor sleeping while Ares flew, Ares sleeping while Gregor kept watch, until finally Gregor awoke to the words, "Overlander, we are here."

They were not moving. Gregor sat up and rubbed his eyes. The light was brighter than any he'd encountered for days. He slid off Ares's back onto a polished stone floor and looked around. They were in the High Hall. It was completely empty. Somewhere, not too far away, he could hear music playing.

"Where is everybody?" asked Gregor.

"I do not know. But if there is music, there must be some sort of gathering," replied Ares. "I believe it is coming from the Throne Room."

They shuffled along a few corridors and came to the doorway of a huge room that Gregor had never seen before. The floor sloped down slightly, like a movie theater, and was filled with rows and rows of stone benches. The place was packed with bats and humans, who were dressed a lot fancier than usual. Many people held objects wrapped in cloth and tied with ribbons. Presents, maybe? Everyone's attention was on a large stone throne at the far end of the room. Nerissa was sitting on the throne.

They had cleaned her up for the occasion. Her unkempt hair had been worked into elaborate braids and piled on top of her head. A jewel-trimmed gown hung loosely off her bony shoulders. Vikus stood behind her. He was reciting some sort of speech as he lowered a large gold crown onto her head. It was hard to imagine either Nerissa or Vikus looking sadder than they did at this moment.

"What's going on?" whispered Gregor.

"A coronation. They are crowning Nerissa queen," Ares said softly.

Luxa had been right. If she died, Nerissa would be crowned, and not Vikus, and his family. At least, not yet.

"So I guess Howard and those guys got back," said Gregor. How else would they know that Luxa was dead?

"So it would seem," said Ares.

If Mareth had survived, he would be down in the hospital, but Howard and Andromeda should be here. Gregor looked around the hall but couldn't find them.

Vikus finished speaking just as he settled the crown

on Nerissa's head and released it. Her thin neck bent forward under the weight, and Gregor thought how ill-suited she was to be queen of this violent, warring place. Whether she was mentally unstable or actually could see the future wasn't the issue. The girl was too weak to hold up her head with a crown on it. The image of Luxa shoving back her gold band flashed before Gregor's eyes. Whether she wanted to be queen or not, there was no doubt in his mind she would have been up to the job. But she was gone now.

Howard was right: They should have made Vikus king. Vikus would make a good leader; he was smart and diplomatic. And he did not seem like he would let power go to his head.

As Nerissa braced her hands on the arms of the throne and managed to raise her head, her eyes caught Gregor's. Something registered on her face, and then she fainted dead away, tumbling to the floor. The crown hit the stone with a clank and then rolled off.

There was a big commotion. A stretcher appeared almost immediately, and Nerissa was carried away. There was a lot of head shaking and murmuring in the crowd from the Underlanders who had probably been opposed to Nerissa being made queen in the first place.

Then somebody spotted Gregor and Ares. They had been standing in the doorway, unnoticed, since everyone had been watching the crowning. Now hundreds of faces turned their way and began to shout questions. Gregor could see Vikus waving for him to come down. This wasn't really how he would have chosen to reveal the story about the Bane. He had planned to tell Vikus, alone, and then head home. But that option was gone.

As Gregor and Ares made their way down the aisle to Vikus, the crowd parted and gradually grew silent. By the time they'd reached the throne it was as if everyone was holding their breath.

"Greetings, Gregor the Overlander, Ares, we are happy to see you alive. What news do you bring us?" asked Vikus. "Did you find the Bane?"

"We found it," said Gregor.

The Underlanders broke into chatter. Vikus motioned for them to be quiet. "And did you drain its light?" he asked.

"No, we took it to Ripred," Gregor said.

There was a moment of disbelief, and then the crowd went crazy. He could see the faces, human and bat alike, twist into fury. Something hit him on the side of his head. His hand went up and came away bloody. A small, ornate crystal jar was down by his feet. It must have been meant as a present for the new queen. More objects began to rain around him. An ink pot. A medallion. A goblet. The one thing they had in common was that they were all made of stone. Gregor realized that it didn't matter how beautifully the gifts were carved. You could call them works of art, but it didn't change the fact that he and Ares were being stoned to death.

Ares tried to get between Gregor and the mob, but it was no use. It was pressing in, forcing the pair up against the back wall. Voices cried out for their death.

Gregor remembered Ripred's words. "And you know, there will be hell to pay in Regalia." The rat might have been a little more specific!

Through the chaos he heard a horn blowing and then the crowd was falling back. A ring of guards formed a semicircle around them. They were escorted out of the room.

"You will follow," said a woman who seemed in charge, and Gregor did, happy to be getting away from the mob.

They went down flight after flight of steps, and eventually reached a quiet hallway deep under the palace. The woman held a stone door open for them, and

Gregor sensed that this was odd. There were few doors of any kind in the palace.

He and Ares went inside the torchlit room, and the door swung shut behind them. There was the sound of something sliding into place. "Where are we?" he asked Ares. "Is this like a special room to keep us safe?"

"It is to keep others safe from us," said Ares. "This is the dungeon. We have been placed under arrest for high treason."

"What?" said Gregor. "What for?"

"For committing crimes against the state of Regalia," said Ares. "Did you not hear the charge?"

Gregor hadn't heard anything but a bunch of people yelling.

"Oh, man!" He pounded on the door with his fist. "Let me out of here! I want to talk to Vikus!" There was no response. He gave up pretty soon since it really hurt to hit the stone door.

He turned back to Ares. "So, treason, huh? That's great. What happens if we're found guilty? We get banished or something?"

"No, Overlander," said Ares. "The punishment for treason is death."

"Death?" It took Gregor a moment to register. "You mean . . . they're going to kill us for not killing the Bane?"

"If it is determined that it was a treasonous act," said Ares.

"And who decides that?" Gregor asked, hoping it was Vikus.

"A tribunal of judges. The final sentence must be approved by the queen," said Ares.

"Well, Luxa isn't going to let them —" he started. Then he remembered that Nerissa was queen now. No telling what she would do. "Would Nerissa let them kill us?"

"I do not know. I have not seen her since I allowed

her brother to fall to his death," said Ares. "I could not face her."

Gregor slid down the wall and sat clumsily on the ground, overwhelmed. He had risked so much, lost so much for these people, and now they were going to kill him?

"I am sorry, Overlander. I should not have brought you back to Regalia. I should have foreseen this would be a possibility," said Ares. "This is all my fault."

"It's not your fault," said Gregor.

"I thought there was a very good chance we would be banished, but then I could have flown you home. I am as good as banished, anyway, so what matter? But treason . . . I did not think they would take it this far. They have never put an Overlander on trial before, and certainly not one so young." Ares began to rock back and forth. He seemed to be talking more to himself than to Gregor. "I cannot let this happen! I have already lost one bond; whatever his intentions, it does not change the fact that I let Henry die. I will not lose the Overlander, I will not let him be — wait! I have a plan!" Ares turned to Gregor, his eyes darting around as the plan took shape. "I will tell them that this was all my idea. That I would not let you kill the Bane . . .

I . . . I . . . stole your sword . . . yes! That will work because you came home without one. And then I forced you to take the Bane to Ripred because I am in a league with the rats. They will believe this . . . I am much hated and deeply distrusted here already!"

Gregor stared at Ares in disbelief. Did Ares actually think he would agree to that? "I'm not going to let you do that! I mean, just the opposite happened. I'm the one who wouldn't kill the Bane and I'm the one who wanted to take it to Ripred. If anyone should be cleared, it's you."

"But it will not help me, Overlander. I will die no matter what. This is what they all want. We may still be able to save you. Think of your family," Ares pleaded.

Gregor did, and it was awful. First Boots, now him. But he couldn't throw Ares to the lions that way. His family wouldn't want him to lie and get Ares killed for something he'd done. "No," said Gregor.

"But you —" Ares began.

"No," said Gregor. "I'm not doing it, Ares."

"Then we will both die!" Ares said angrily.

"Then we will!" They sat there, both of them stewing for a minute. "So, how do they do it?" asked Gregor.

"You will not like it," said Ares.

"Well, probably not. But I'd rather know," said Gregor.

"They will bind my wings and your hands and drop us off a very high cliff to the rocks below," said Ares.

It was Gregor's recurring nightmare. For as long as he could remember he'd had terrible dreams about it. Falling through space . . . smashing into the ground . . . it was how Henry had died. And King Gorger's rats. He had heard their screams as they fell, had seen their bodies bursting open on the rocks.

For a moment, he was tempted to take Ares up on his offer. But he couldn't.

A small hatch at the base of the dungeon door swung open, and two bowls of food were pushed in. The hatch slammed shut.

It seemed impossible to eat at a time like this, but Gregor's stomach began to growl at the smell of food. "You want to eat?" he asked Ares.

"I suppose we should to keep up our strength," said the bat. "Some opportunity for escape may arise."

The bowls contained some kind of porridge and a chunk of bread. It wasn't the most exciting meal on earth, but after days of raw fish, it tasted great. Gregor wolfed his down and felt a little better. Just because they were accused of something didn't mean they'd been found guilty. Maybe when the tribunal heard his version of what had happened, they would understand. And then there was Nerissa . . .

"So no matter what the tribunal decides, Nerissa can keep us alive if she wants to?" asked Gregor.

"Yes, she can spare our lives. But Overlander, I let Henry die," said Ares.

"Yeah, but you know what she told me? She told me she thought it was best that he died. Because if he hadn't, everybody else would have died, too," said Gregor.

"Did she?" said Ares. "It must have taken many dark nights to come to that conclusion."

"Does she really see things? I mean, like the future?" said Gregor.

"Yes, she does. I have witnessed it. But she is young, and her gift is a torture to her. She sees many things she does not understand, and many things that frighten her. At times she doubts her own sanity," said Ares.

Gregor didn't respond to that. He wasn't convinced that she was sane, either.

The door swung open, and the guards stepped in. "It is time for your hearing," said the one in charge.

His hopes for escape dimmed when they bound his hands behind his back. Ares's wings were pinned against his body with a rope. It was like they were already being prepared for the execution. All they needed was the cliff.

Several guards hoisted Ares onto their shoulders and marched off briskly. Gregor followed behind as they retraced their steps up several flights from the dungeon and then veered off to another part of the palace.

They entered a room that was set up for judgment. This was not the room where the Underlanders had threatened to banish Ares. It was more formal. More official. A long, stone table with three chairs sat at the front. "That's for the judges," Gregor thought. Directly behind the center chair, elevated by a platform was a throne. Off to the right, as you faced the table, was a stone cube with three steps going up to it. It was positioned so that not only the judges but anyone sitting in the seven tiers of seats that rose to the high ceilings could get a good view of it. The witness stand.

Every seat in the house was filled with either a bat or a human. They stared down at Gregor and Ares with undisguised hatred, but it was eerily quiet. It had almost been better when everybody was screaming and throwing stuff.

Gregor was directed to an open area in front of the table. The guards set Ares down next to him. They stood staring at the empty table before them. Then there was the sound of more footsteps. Gregor turned his head and found Howard and Andromeda behind him. They were both bound and looked ragged.

"What are you doing here?" Gregor exclaimed.

"We, too, are on trial for treason," Howard said hoarsely.

"For what?" said Gregor. "You never even made it to the Bane!"

"That is precisely the reason," said Howard.

Then Gregor realized what he meant. Howard and Andromeda were on trial because they had not finished their mission; they had returned to Regalia with Mareth.

"But," objected Gregor, "I made you go back!"

"No one made me do anything," said Howard. "I came back of my own free will."

"Well, that's not what I'm saying," said Gregor. He

was suddenly overwhelmed by the way his decision had jeopardized the lives of those who had fought by his side. He couldn't let this happen.

A side door opened, and an old man and a decrepit white bat entered. A moment later an elderly woman appeared with several scrolls. All three took seats at the table. The woman, who seemed to be the head judge, took the center seat. She glanced back at the throne and addressed a guard.

"May we expect Queen Nerissa?" she asked.

"They are checking now to see if she has regained consciousness, your honor," said the guard.

The woman nodded, but Gregor could hear people in the crowd murmuring, probably about the frailty of their new queen. One glance from the head judge and the room fell silent. Gregor had the feeling that whoever she was, his life was in her hands.

For a few minutes, nothing much happened. The judges preoccupied themselves with examining the scrolls.

Gregor shifted his weight slightly from side to side. The rope was really biting into his wrists. He wondered if he could ask them to cut it loose or if that would be a major breach of court behavior. Well, it was worth a try.

"Excuse me, your honor?" he said. The judges all looked at him in surprise.

"Yes, Overlander?" said the woman.

"Do you think you could untie us now? I'm losing all the feeling in my fingers," said Gregor. "And they knotted the rope right over one of my squid-sucker sores. You can't see it, but Ares's whole back is covered with open wounds from those flesh-eating mites that killed Pandora. And Howard and Andromeda are pretty beat up, too."

Even if she said no, Gregor was still glad he'd spoken. He wanted them to know — all these idiots packing the seats, waiting for his death sentence — that he and Ares and Howard and Andromeda were the ones who had been out risking their lives. Suddenly he couldn't wait to testify.

"Cut free the defendants," the head judge said, and turned back to her scroll.

No one in the crowd dared object. A guard cut all their bonds. Gregor rubbed his wrists and glanced back to see that Howard was doing the same.

"Did Mareth make it?" he asked.

Howard's tormented face broke into a brief smile. "Yes. He will mend."

"I can't believe you kept him alive after that serpent attack!" said Gregor. He said "serpent attack" extra loud to make sure everyone heard, then turned back to the front before anyone could tell him to shut up.

A guard hurried into the room and whispered something to the head judge.

"Very well," said the head judge. "We will begin." She cleared her throat and read off the series of charges against the defendants. The language was pretty complicated, but it all seemed to boil down to the fact that Gregor hadn't killed the Bane, and nobody else had, either.

The head judge finished the list of charges and looked up. "We will now question those on trial."

"Can I go first?" It burst out of Gregor before he could stop it, but suddenly he knew he had to. He could sense that Howard, Ares, and probably Andromeda were already convinced they were guilty. If they got up on the stand, they might not be able to defend themselves. He, on the other hand, was absolutely bubbling over with the injustice of the whole thing.

"Overlander," the head judge said firmly, "it is not our custom to shout out inquiries during a trial, especially one so serious in nature."

"Sorry," Gregor said, but he didn't hang his head or look away. "What should I do if I have a question, raise my hand? I mean, I don't have a lawyer or anything, right?"

"Raising your hand should be sufficient," the head judge said, ignoring his lawyer question.

He thought about raising his hand and asking if he could go first again. But that might seem snotty. Whether it was because he had asked or because he was already slated to do so, Gregor was called directly to the stand. He climbed the steps to the cube. It was designed so people could see any twitch, any shift in the defendant's body language. He felt very exposed.

Gregor expected to be bombarded with questions, like you saw on TV, but the judges merely settled back in their seats and looked at him.

"Tell us, then," said the head judge. "Tell us about your journey."

This threw him a little. "Where . . . where do you want me to start?"

"Start from the day you sailed away from Regalia," said the head judge.

So, he did. He told his story. And every chance he got, he made sure to emphasize the courage the others on trial had shown. When he got to the part at the Tankard, he said, "I made Howard leave. He didn't have any choice. I was going to fight him if he tried to come with us. I'd have fought Andromeda, too, she knew that. That's why they went home. How could they risk injuring me when I still had to kill the Bane?"

"And why did you not want them to accompany you?" said the old bat judge.

Gregor had a moment of confusion. "Because . . . I don't know . . . because we needed to get Mareth back, for one thing. And I didn't want a whole bunch of people in that maze, I guess. I wanted my family to know what had happened to my sister . . . and me, if I didn't come back. And because . . . because . . ." He spun back in his mind to the cave, to the ice that had engulfed him. "Because the Bane was mine."

A gasp rose from the crowd at his insolence.

"What do you mean, the Bane was yours?" asked the bat.

"It was mine to kill. That's what your prophecy says, right? I'm the guy who's supposed to kill it? In the end, it was always my job," said Gregor. "And it was my call, who I wanted to take into that maze — not yours." He paused. "Anyway, if you kill Howard and Andromeda because they came back, that's just murder. Nobody could have done better than they did."

He looked over to where the others stood. It was hard to read Andromeda, but she did shake her wings a little. Howard's lips silently formed a couple of words. Gregor was pretty sure they were "thank you." Maybe he'd made a convincing enough argument to keep them alive.

"Go on with your story. What happened after your company parted ways?" asked the head judge.

Gregor took a deep breath. This part was going to be harder. He told about entering the Labyrinth, having to leave Twitchtip behind, finding the cone, and witnessing the bloody fight between Goldshard and Snare. There was a reaction from the crowd again. Gregor suspected they were happy that Snare was dead.

Just then Nerissa appeared in the doorway, leaning heavily on Vikus's arm. Her coronation gown was lopsided, and stray braids hung out of her hairdo. There was not even the suggestion of a crown — no tiara, no gold band — on her head. She kept squinting, as if she were in bright sunlight.

It took Vikus and a pair of guards to help her up onto the throne. She swayed slightly, even when she was seated, as if at any moment she might plunge to the ground.

"Queen Nerissa, are you well enough to attend this trial?" the head judge asked in a neutral tone.

"Oh, yes," said Nerissa. "I have seen myself here before, although I do not know the outcome."

This was the sort of stuff that made everybody think she was crazy. Maybe someone ought to tell her to keep her visions under her hat. Crown. Whatever.

"The charge is treason?" Nerissa said doubtfully, and Gregor realized she had no idea what was going on.

The head judge said slowly, "Yes, the defendants are on trial for treason."

Nerissa stared at an empty spot on the wall for a moment, then shook her head. "Forgive me. I have only just awoken."

"Do you wish us to begin the proceedings again?" asked the head judge.

"Oh, no, please continue," said Nerissa. She knotted up her hands in her skirt, hiking it up above her knees. Another braid sprang free from its pins and fell down the side of her face. Her whole body was shaking.

The head judge looked over at Vikus, who avoided her gaze and busied himself placing his cloak around Nerissa's shoulders.

The queen gave him a smile. "I wish I had some soup."

"Oh, geez," thought Gregor. She wasn't going to help their case any.

The head judge turned to Gregor. "So, after the fight between the gnawers, Goldshard and Snare. What occurred next?"

Gregor tried to regain his focus. "So, then, we heard a scratching in one of the tunnels, and we knew it was the Bane. But the tunnel was small; Ares couldn't fit into it. I had to leave him in the cone. I went down the tunnel; I was ready to kill it. Then when I found the Bane, it started crying and calling, 'Mama,' and I mean — you told me it was like this ten-foot rat! I guess you didn't know, or whatever, but I wasn't expecting the Bane to be a baby."

Nerissa flew to her feet. "A baby!"

"Yeah, it was a baby rat," Gregor said, surprised she was even following along.

She stumbled down the steps and came reeling around the table, her skirt still twisted up in one hand while the other waved wildly. "Oh, Warrior! Oh, Warrior!" she cried frantically. As she lurched toward him, he was torn between trying to catch her and just getting out of the way. Right before she made it to the cube, he leaped off and grabbed her by the shoulders. The icy fingers of her free hand clutched the neck of his shirt.

"Oh, you did not kill it, did you?" she said.

"No, Nerissa, I didn't kill it," he said, totally baffled. "I couldn't."

She heaved a huge, shuddering sigh and sank down to the ground at his feet, laughing in relief. "Oh . . . oh . . ." She patted his knee reassuringly. "Then we may all yet be saved."

CHAPTER

26

She sat on the floor rocking back and forth laughing, the very picture of madness.

"Man, somebody needs to help this girl," thought Gregor.

Vikus came up and crouched beside her on the floor. "Nerissa, perhaps you should rest longer. Are you feeling ill?"

"Oh, no, I am well. We are all well!" giggled Nerissa. "The warrior has fulfilled the prophecy."

"No, Nerissa, he did not succeed in killing the Bane," Vikus said gently.

"Vikus," said Nerissa. "The baby lives. So lives the warrior's heart. The gnawers do *not* have their key to power."

Vikus looked like a lightning bolt had hit him. He plunked down on the floor next to her. "This is what Sandwich meant?" he said. "We never considered it."

"What?" said Gregor. He wasn't sure what was going on.

"The baby in the prophecy was never your sister, Gregor. It was the Bane," said Vikus.

"The Bane? Why would it kill my heart if the Bane died?" said Gregor.

"Why did you not drain its light?" asked Vikus.

"Because it's a baby. It's just wrong," said Gregor. "It's the most evil thing . . . I . . . I mean, if you can kill a baby, what can't you do?"

"So says your heart. So says your most essential part," said Nerissa.

Gregor took a few steps back and sat on the cube. Nerissa's meaning was slowly dawning on him.

DIE THE BABY, DIE HIS HEART,
DIE HIS MOST ESSENTIAL PART.

His most essential part was the part that had spared the Bane. If he had killed it, he would have never been the same. He would have lost himself forever.

"You know," Vikus said to Nerissa, as if they were the only two in the room, "I am continually amazed by how badly we can interpret one of Sandwich's prophecies. Then the moment it is understood —"

"The whole thing is as clear as water," agreed Nerissa.

Vikus quoted a section from the prophecy:

WHAT COULD TURN THE WARRIOR WEAK?
WHAT DO BURNING GNAWERS SEEK?
JUST A BARELY SPEAKING PUP
WHO HOLDS THE LAND OF UNDER UP.

"The gnawers have always sought the Bane . . . ," said Vikus.

"Who is just a barely speaking pup. Sandwich even went so far as to use the word 'pup.' The gnawers' own word for baby," said Nerissa.

"And the Bane holds the land of Under up," nodded Vikus.

"Because if Gregor had killed it . . . ," continued Nerissa.

"Total war," said Vikus. "Its death would have been enough to rally them. Taking that pup to Ripred was a stroke of genius, Gregor. Oh, they will not know how to parry that move."

"Queen Nerissa, are we to continue this trial?" asked the head judge.

Nerissa looked up, as if she was surprised at her surroundings. "Trial? For the warrior? Of course there will be no trial! He has saved the Underland." She got to her feet, using Vikus for support, and saw the other defendants staring at her. She gave them a small smile, but directed her next line to Ares. "And all who helped him are held in our highest regard."

Ares ducked his head. Maybe it was a bow or maybe he couldn't look at her.

"Will you dine with me, you four? You look half-starved," said Nerissa. It was kind of ironic coming from her, but a welcome invitation.

Somewhat dazed by the recent turn of events, Gregor, Ares, Howard, and Andromeda straggled out of the courtroom after Nerissa. She led them to a small, private dining room. The table could seat no more than six. In one corner, water trickled in a fountain. Old tapestries hung on the walls. Gregor guessed the first Underlanders must have brought them from above, because they depicted scenes from the Overland, not this dark world. It was a calming place.

"It's nice in here," said Gregor.

"Yes," said Nerissa. "This is where I often take my meals."

They all took seats. People brought in platters of elegant food. Large fish stuffed with grain and herbs, tiny vegetables arranged in geometric patterns, steaming braided bread studded with fruit, paper-thin piles of roast beef, and Ripred's favorite, that shrimp in cream sauce. Heaping plates were placed in front of each of them.

"Do not suppose I always dine so sumptuously," said Nerissa. "This food was prepared for the coronation. Please, begin."

Gregor lifted his bread, dipped it in the cream sauce, and took a big bite.

For a while, they all concentrated on the food. Except Nerissa, who seemed to be mostly rearranging hers.

"I am afraid I am a poor conversationalist," said Nerissa. "Even at my best. And at present, grief for my cousin's fate has robbed me of what little I might venture to say."

"It is the same for all of us," Howard said sadly.

"Yes, no one here has been spared," said Nerissa.

It was true. The journey to the Labyrinth had given them all ample reason for grief. Gregor was glad that Nerissa acknowledged it and that they could continue in silence.

After days of insufficient food, Gregor's stomach was soon heavy with the rich dishes before him. The others stopped eating as well. You would think they'd all be shoveling down seven or eight helpings, but it didn't work that way.

Nerissa then sent the four of them down to the hospital. Andromeda and Howard hadn't received medical care or been allowed a bath, either.

"When did you guys get back?" asked Gregor.

"About twelve hours before you arrived. Andromeda was astonishing. She barely rested at all. When we landed, they took Mareth to the hospital, and locked us up. But I knew one of our guards. She whispered word of Mareth's recovery to us," said Howard.

At the hospital, all four of them were immediately sent to bathe. Gregor realized he must be knocking people over with the rotten-egg smell. After several days, he didn't much notice it anymore. He sank into a tub and felt all his injuries object. The squid-sucker marks on his arm, the aching ribs, the bump on his head from Ripred, the various abrasions and bruises from the stoning, the rope burns around his wrists. Wincing, he scrubbed himself down. It was lucky that the bathwater was continually carried away by the current. It would have been the color of mud by the time he was through.

The doctors treated his wounds. He spoke only when they asked him a direct question about an injury. When he finished, the others were waiting for him.

"I suppose we should all get some rest," said Howard.

"Is that safe?" asked Gregor.

No one answered. Their status in Regalia was foggy. Nerissa had cleared them, but Gregor had a feeling plenty of people still thought they were guilty.

"I have a large chamber that would accommodate us. It is reserved for my family at all times," said Howard. "At least we know we are safe with one another."

They all followed Howard back to his room. Gregor was glad he had offered. He didn't want to go back to the room he had always shared with Boots here.

"Where's your family?" asked Gregor.

"They returned to the Fount a few days after we left. I expect they are trying to travel here now, as I am . . . as I was on trial for treason," said Howard.

Howard's family actually had several chambers reserved for them. It was like a small apartment of connecting rooms. But they all gathered to sleep in one that the kids shared. Howard and Gregor took beds next to each other. Ares and Andromeda huddled together in the space between them.

"To sleep, then," said Howard.

The bats dropped off almost instantly. Howard tossed and turned awhile, but then Gregor could hear his breathing slow down and become rhythmic. He lay in bed wishing sleep would carry him away. But it wouldn't come.

What would happen now? He guessed he would be allowed to go home. Probably pretty soon. Then there would be his family to face. And life without Boots. It still wasn't quite real. It would be, when he was back in the apartment, looking at her bed, her toys, her cardboard box of books.

Gregor thought of her clothes sitting in the museum. He didn't want to leave them here for people to poke through. He grabbed a torch·off the wall and left Howard's room.

A few guards saw him along the way, but no one tried to stop him. Nor did they greet him or say anything. He had the feeling they didn't know how they were supposed to treat him, so they left him alone.

He found the museum on his own. There, by the door, was the little pile of Boots's clothes. He pressed her shirt against his nose and could smell that sweet combination of shampoo and peanut butter and baby that was his sister. For the first time, his eyes welled up with tears.

"Gregor?" said a voice behind him.

He stuffed the shirt in the pack and wiped his eyes as Vikus came into the museum.

"Hey, Vikus," he said. "What's up?"

"The council has just adjourned what I believe to be the first of many meetings addressing 'The Prophecy of Bane.' I am convinced Nerissa's interpretation is correct, but there is dissension. This is to be expected, as it is a new idea. But until it is decided, her word stands. As that could change, I think it best if you leave here as soon as possible."

"Fine by me," said Gregor. "What about the others?"

"I believe charges will not be reinstated against Andromeda and Howard. Your testimony of their innocence was quite convincing," said Vikus.

"And Ares?" said Gregor.

Vikus sighed. "He is at greater risk. But if he is to be charged again, I will get word to him so that he may flee. He can at least escape execution."

Gregor nodded. That was about as much as he could hope for.

"Is there anything you would like to take back with you?" Vikus asked, gesturing to the shelves.

"I don't want anything but our stuff," said Gregor.

"If not for yourself, perhaps for your parents," said Vikus. "How does your father . . . does he teach again?"

"No, he's still too sick," said Gregor.

"How so?" Vikus asked, frowning.

Gregor choked out a list of his dad's symptoms. His father's health was just one more thing the Underland had stolen from them.

Vikus tried to question him in more detail, but he couldn't take it. "You know, maybe I will take that clock," he said, pointing to the cuckoo clock he had seen when he was collecting batteries. He had said it to change the subject, but he knew someone who might like it.

"I will have it wrapped for you," said Vikus.

"Great, so I guess I'll see if Ares is up for flying yet, and like you said, get out of here," said Gregor. He scooped up his clothes and left the museum. Vikus could learn a thing or two from Nerissa. Sometimes people just didn't want to talk.

He got all turned around on his way back to Howard's room. The route was unfamiliar, and the tears that had started back in the museum were streaming down his cheeks. Well, maybe it was better to break down here than in front of his parents. He turned left, then right, then backtracked. Where was he? Where was his sister? She had just been here, he had her clothes, he could feel her in his arms . . . Boots!

He gave up and pressed his forehead into a stone wall, sobbing as he let the pain in. Images of her swarmed back into his mind. Boots on the sled . . . Boots showing him how she could hop on one foot . . . Boots's eyes, upside down, their foreheads pressed together. . . .

TWO ROWS
TINY, TINY TOES

Boots ten . . . wiggle my nose
Whew!

He could even hear her voice trying to do the silly bath rhyme Howard had coaxed her out of her tears with.

Wiggle nose
Nine, ten toes

She couldn't get it right. The words were too complicated. . . .

Give them bath so ten toes goes.

And then she gave a sneeze.

Gregor looked up. That didn't make sense. He heard a second sneeze. Not in his head. In the palace. He started to run.

Two rows
Tiny, tiny toes

Either he was completely losing it . . .

. . . or that sound was real! He flew down the halls, crashing into walls and a couple of guards who called for him to halt. He didn't.

Wiggle nose
Nine, ten toes

Gregor ran into the room just in time for the last line.

Give them bath so ten toes goes.

She was sitting on the floor, surrounded by six big cockroaches, rubbing her toes with both hands to show how she washed them. He stumbled across the room and grabbed her up in his arms and held on tight as a happy voice squeaked in his ear.

"Hi, you!"

CHAPTER

27

"Hi, you," Gregor said, thinking he would never let go of her. "Oh, hi, you! Where've you been, little girl?"

"I go swim, I go ride. Flutterfly," said Boots.

"Okay, all right," laughed Gregor. "That sounds great." He'd have to ask the others what happened. "Hey, Temp," he said, turning to the roaches, and then he realized something was wrong. Before him stood six roaches with two perfect antennas each and six solid legs. Maybe he was finally learning to tell them apart, because he knew, anyway, that none of them was Temp.

"Where's Temp?" he asked, and six pairs of antennas drooped.

"We do not know, not we," said one of the roaches. "I be Pend, I be."

Gregor turned in a full circle, just to be sure. It was the room where you could ride the platform down to the ground. Temp wasn't there. Neither were Luxa and Aurora. He tightened his grip on Boots.

About this time, Vikus came hurrying into the room, followed by several guards. His face lit up when he saw Boots. "They have returned!" he said to Gregor.

"Just Boots, Vikus. I'm sorry," Gregor said, and watched the color drain out of the old man's face.

Vikus turned to the roaches. "Welcome, Pend. Many thanks for the return of the princess. Tell us, will you, tell us the fate of the others?"

Pend tried to fill him in, but the roaches knew very little. A moth — that must have been Boots's flutterfly — had arrived in their land carrying Boots. It had been flying in the Dead Land when it had discovered the little girl and Temp hiding in the rocks. Temp was very weak and unable to travel farther. He begged the moth to take Boots back to the other crawlers. Since the moths and cockroaches were allies, the moth had agreed. When the crawlers sent a party back to rescue Temp, he was nowhere to be found.

"Did they make any mention of my granddaughter?" asked Vikus. "Queen Luxa?"

"Run you, Queen Luxa said, run you," said Pend. "Many gnawers, there were. Temp said no more."

Vikus reached out and fumbled with Boots's hair. "Temp seepy," she said. "He shut eyes. I ride flutterfly." She looked around. "Where Temp?"

"He's still sleeping, Boots," said Gregor. Sleeping like Tick was sleeping, probably.

"Shh," Boots said, putting her finger to her lips.

Someone had wakened Dulcet. When she tried to take Boots out of Gregor's arms, he resisted. "It is all right, Gregor. I will bathe her and bring her back directly," said Dulcet. Since it was Dulcet, he made his hands let go.

He followed Vikus to the dining room, where they'd last eaten with Ripred, and they both took a seat. Gregor tried to piece it together in his head.

"It seems," Vikus said at last, "they did not perish in the Tankard."

"No," said Gregor. "But Twitchtip was sure there was water between us, and they didn't answer Ares."

After a while, Dulcet came in with a clean and shiny Boots. Vikus sent for food. Gregor held her on his lap while she gobbled up enough dinner for ten toddlers.

"Boots," said Gregor, "you know when we saw the big . . ." He didn't know what to call those things. "Serpents" wasn't a word she knew. "Those big dinosaurs."

"I no like," said Boots. "I no like dinosaws."

"Me, either," said Gregor. "But remember when we saw them. And they knocked us off the bat. And Luxa caught you and Temp. Where did you go?"

"Oh, I swim. Too cold. I bump head," Boots said, rubbing the top of her head.

Gregor separated her curls with his fingers. He could see little scrape marks on the delicate skin of her scalp. Where had she been? Not in the Tankard. "Was it a big pool, Boots?"

"Baby pool," said Boots. "I bump head."

Gregor suddenly remembered the tunnel Twitchtip had been guiding them to. The one half under water. If Luxa had dived for that tunnel and made it, the entrance soon would have been flooded with the waves churned up by the serpents. Maybe that was the water between them. At some point they all must have been floating in water, or Boots wouldn't have said she'd been swimming. How had they kept from drowning?

Then he remembered the life jackets. Boots was not wearing hers when she came in, but she had had it on at the Tankard.

He told his theory to Vikus. "Yes, something of that nature must have occurred. But then they would have been trapped in the Labyrinth," said Vikus. "Boots, did you see rats?"

Boots put her hand to her nose. "Ow," she said. At first Gregor thought she had hurt her nose, but when she said, "Bandidge. No touch. I no touch it. Ow," he knew.

"Twitchtip found them. Or they found her," he said. "Was it Twitchtip, Boots? With the bandage?"

"I no touch. Ow," Boots confirmed, pressing her nose.

"And then what happened, Boots?" asked Gregor. "What did you do with Twitchtip? Did you see more rats?"

"Temp give Boots ride. Fast ride!" Boots said, but that was all they could get out of her.

"They were attacked, no doubt, by gnawers. Luxa told Temp to run with Boots, then stayed to fight with Aurora and perhaps Twitchtip," said Vikus. "I am sure their odds were not good."

Gregor was sure their odds had been next to zero, but he tried to be encouraging. "Well, if they had Twitchtip, they could get out of the maze, Vikus. Or maybe the rats wanted to keep them alive and took them prisoner. Like they did my dad. I mean, she's a queen, she's important."

Maybe Gregor shouldn't have said that, because the idea of what the rats might do to Luxa if she was their prisoner was almost scarier than thinking of her dead. He thought of his dad, waking up screaming from nightmares . . .

Vikus nodded, but his eyes shone with tears.

"The point is . . . the point is . . . we don't know," said Gregor. "A lot of things could have happened to them. And remember the gift you wanted to give me? The last time I was here?"

"Hope," whispered Vikus.

"Yeah. Don't give that up yet, okay?" said Gregor.

"I done," Boots said, pushing her plate off the table and watching with satisfaction as it banged to the floor. "I done."

"Well, if you are done, Boots, how would you like to go home?" said Vikus.

"Ye-es!" said Boots. "I go home!"

"I can stay, Vikus. Or I can take Boots home and come back and help you look for Luxa and —" Gregor started, but Vikus cut him off.

"No, Gregor. No. If they are dead, there is nothing any of us can do. If they are held prisoner, it will likely be months before we can locate them. In that time, who knows? They could reverse Nerissa's verdict and execute you. If I have need of you, believe me, I will find some way to send for you," said Vikus. "For now, you must go home. You have worries of your own there, yes?"

Well, yes. Gregor had worries wherever he was.

In about half an hour they were down on the dock, dressed in their own clothes, climbing on Ares's back. The only ones who had come to see them off were Vikus, Andromeda, Howard, and Nerissa.

"Give my best to Mareth," Gregor said to Andromeda.

"Yes, Overlander. He would wish you well also," said the bat.

Gregor turned to Howard. "If you hear anything about Luxa and the others, let me know. My laundry room's right at the top of one of those gateways. Ares knows which one. Leave me a note or something, okay?"

"I will get word to you," said Howard.

To his surprise, Nerissa tucked a scroll in his coat pocket. "The prophecy. So you can reflect on it sometimes."

Gregor shook his head. "I don't think I can forget it, Nerissa. But thanks." What did she think he was going to do? Take it home and frame it?

Vikus handed him a flashlight, a large package in the shape of a cuckoo clock, and a silk bag that held a heavy stone jar. "Medicine," he said. "For your father. The instructions are written inside."

"Oh, good!" said Gregor. Maybe they had something down here that could cure his dad. He gave Vikus a hug. "Hang in there, okay, Vikus?"

"Yes. Fly you high, Gregor the Overlander," said Vikus.

"Fly you high," said Gregor.

"See you soon!" Boots said as they took off, but there was no response from the dock. Last time, he had been horrified to think that they would ever return. Now, with Luxa and the others on his mind, he felt reluctant to leave.

"You let me know!" he called to them, but if anyone answered, he couldn't hear them.

Ares carried them down the river, across the Waterway, up through the tunnels, and back to the foot of the steep staircase that led to Central Park. He climbed off the bat's back with Boots.

"You going to be okay?" he asked Ares.

"As well as you," said Ares. "Fly you high, Gregor the Overlander."

Gregor lifted his hand to grasp Ares's extended claw. "Fly you high, Ares the Flier."

Ares took off into the dark of the tunnel, and Gregor and Boots headed up the stairs.

It took a little while to move the rock — it had frozen into place — but finally Gregor was able to wiggle it loose. It was night. The park was empty. Lamplight shone down on the foot of snow that covered the ground. It was beautiful.

"Sedding? We go sedding?" asked Boots.

"Not now, Boots," said Gregor. "Maybe another time." If he could find another park with a hill. He'd never bring her back here.

They caught a taxi. New York City was ablaze with Christmas decorations and lights. "Do you know the date today?" he asked the driver, who tapped on a cheap block calendar on the dashboard. December 23. They hadn't missed it. They would all be home for Christmas. And that idea, which had been so impossible a few hours before, made him feel like the luckiest person alive.

Boots snuggled up under his arm and gave a big yawn. Boots . . . the Bane . . . right now they were so alike that the entire Underland could misinterpret the prophecy and mistake them for each other. But what would happen when the Bane grew up in a year or so? Would it become the monster predicted in the prophecy, or an entirely different creature? He hoped Ripred would do a good job raising it.

Although even if Ripred did all the right things, it might be out of his control. Gregor's parents were great, and here he was, a rager. He was going to have to be very, very careful not to get into any fights now that he was home. He wished he'd talked to Ripred more about their condition. "Next time I go down there —" Gregor thought, and a jolt went through him. Because he suddenly knew there would be a next time. He was too tied up in the Underland now, there was too much he cared about: finding Luxa and Aurora and Temp and Twitchtip, if they were still alive; protecting Ares; helping the friends who had helped him.

Gregor paid the driver from the last of the money Mrs. Cormaci had given him.

The elevator was out of order, so he hauled Boots up the stairs. They came through the front door and made it about three steps into the room before his dad caught them in his arms. In minutes, the whole apartment was up. His mom was kissing him, Lizzie was swinging on his hand, his grandma was calling from the bedroom. A million questions were flying at him, but he must have looked whipped, because his mom took his face between her hands and said, "Gregor, you need to go to bed, baby?" And that was exactly what he needed.

The next morning he told the whole story. He softened some of the bad parts, because everybody looked so scared. "But it's okay. Boots wasn't the baby. It was the Bane. So there's no reason the rats would want her now," said Gregor.

"I not baby. I big girl," said Boots, who was sitting on her dad's lap, lining up little plastic animals along the arm of the couch. "I ride bat. I swim. Temp seepy. I tell flutterfly tiny, tiny toes."

"And what about you, Gregor?" said his mother.

"Well, I had my chance to kill the Bane and I didn't do it, so I don't think the rats will come looking for me." He didn't tell her that the Regalians might. "Oh, hey, look what I brought for Mrs. Cormaci. It's a clock. She's been so nice and all, and you know how she loves all those old clocks —"

Gregor pulled open the pack, and a cloud of money floated out. Confused, he emptied the pack on the sofa. There was the clock, all right. But Vikus had ordered them to pack it in money. All those wallets in the museum must be a lot lighter now, because there were literally thousands of dollars in cash on the sofa.

"Oh, my goodness," said his grandma. "Now, what are we going to do with all that?"

"We're going to pay off the bills," his mom said grimly. Her face softened. "And then, we're going to have Christmas."

And they did. They had to rush around like crazy to pull it together, what with Christmas being the very next day, but who cared? Gregor, Lizzie, and their mom went shopping. His grandma and Boots watched Christmas specials on TV, while his dad cleaned up Mrs. Cormaci's cuckoo clock.

Even after the money had been set aside for the bills, there was plenty for Christmas. First they took the old metal laundry cart out and loaded it up with groceries. For a few weeks, anyway, Gregor would not have to feel tense when he opened the kitchen cabinets. Then the guy on the corner who sold trees gave them one half-price, since he was about done for the season, anyway. Lizzie stayed home to help decorate the tree, while Gregor and his mom shopped for presents. He had a hard time getting his mom anything that was a surprise since she wouldn't let him out of her sight.

"Mom, it's not like some giant rat is going to come after me in the middle of Eighty-sixth Street," he said. "There's a million people out."

"You just stay where I can see you," she answered.

He finally managed to get her a pair of earrings while she was buying everybody socks.

That evening, when Mrs. Cormaci came by with an armload of presents for them, Gregor answered the door.

"So, you're finally up and around, Mister," she said.

At first Gregor didn't know what she was talking about; then he remembered he was supposed to have had the flu. "Yeah, that pretty much wiped me out."

"You're thin as a rail," Mrs. Cormaci said, and handed him a plate of Christmas cookies.

Gregor wished he had a picture of her face when she opened the clock. He could tell it blew her away. "Oh, my! Where did you get this?"

There was a pause.

"In one of those places that has old things," said Lizzie.

"An antique shop?" said Mrs. Cormaci.

"Oh, no, just a secondhand place," said his dad. In a way, it was true.

When she left, Gregor carried the clock home for her. She was chattering on about her kids flying in the next day and tickets she'd gotten for some Broadway musical when she stopped short. She was staring at Gregor's feet.

Gregor looked down. The boots were a mess. Badly scarred from Ares's claws, streaked with blood and squid slime, one toe bent in. Before he could think up a story, she spoke.

"Well, looks like you're getting a lot of use out of those," she said.

Gregor didn't answer. He couldn't lie to her again; she had been too good to them.

"You know, one day you're going to realize you can trust me, Gregor," she said.

"I do trust you, Mrs. Cormaci," he mumbled.

"Do you? Flu. Hmph," she said. "I'll see you next Saturday." She shook her head and closed the door.

The tree was decorated, the fridge was packed, the stockings were hung, everyone was in bed except Gregor and his mom. They were wrapping presents in his room. When they were down to the last few, he left her to finish while he tiptoed in to tidy up the living room. His dad was snoring peacefully on the pulled-out sofa — maybe that medicine would help after all. Their coats were in a pile on the floor where Lizzie had dumped them so they could hang their stockings on the coat pegs by the door. As he gathered them up, the cell phone fell out of his coat pocket. He stuffed it back in and felt something.

There, lying flat along the bottom of his jacket pocket, was the prophecy Nerissa had given him. It had been there all day, but he hadn't noticed it. What had she said? He was supposed to reflect on it? He wasn't sure what she'd meant.

Gregor unrolled the scroll and held it in the Christmas tree lights. Something was wrong with the prophecy. It took him a moment to realize it was written backwards.

He traced the title from right to left with his fingers, deciphering the words. "The Prophecy of Bane" — no wait! The last word wasn't "Bane." It was "Blood."

He released the top of the scroll and let it snap shut as his mom came into the room with a big pile of presents.

"You ready for this?" she said.

Gregor slipped the scroll in his back pocket and held out his arms. "Sure," he said. "Ready as I'll ever be."

ACKNOWLEDGMENTS

Many thanks to my terrific agent, Rosemary Stimola, my extraordinary editor, Kate Egan, and Scholastic Press's amazing editorial director, Liz Szabla, who takes such excellent care of Gregor both on the page and in the world. Much appreciation goes also to the wonderful folks at Scholastic, especially Elizabeth Eulberg for being my guide and escort into the land of public appearances.

Special love to my dad, Michael Collins, who passed away last year. He was instrumental in the creation of this series and continues to be at my side as Gregor continues his journey. He will fly with me always. And for my mom, Jane Collins, ongoing gratitude for her thoughtful input and enthusiastic support of these books.

Thanks also to my friends and family for their encouragement, their excitement, and their habit of walking into bookstores around the country and talking up *Gregor the Overlander* in voices too loud to ignore.

Most of all, love to Cap, Charlie, and Isabel, who make it all worthwhile.

ABOUT THE AUTHOR

Suzanne Collins is the author of the ground-breaking Hunger Games trilogy: *The Hunger Games, Catching Fire,* and *Mockingjay.* She is also the author of the *New York Times* bestselling Underland Chronicles, which started with *Gregor the Overlander,* and of *Year of the Jungle,* a picture book. Suzanne lives with her family in Connecticut. You can find her online at suzannecollinsbooks.com.